FIGHTING: CARUSO MAFIA BOOK THREE

Nova Mason

ISBN: 8988974000
ISBN-13: 9798988974000

Cover Design: SelfPubBookCovers.com/billwyc

WARNING:

"Fighting" is the third book in the Caruso Mafia series. While this book can be read as a standalone there are subplots that continue throughout the series, so for the best reading experience, following the suggested reading order. This book is a mafia, second chance romance, complete with HEA and no cliffhangers for the couple.

Please note: this book is a mafia romance that contains mature content, graphic violence and may contain triggers. If such materials offend you, please do not read.

CHAPTER ONE

Seven Years Ago - Val

My time of freedom is nearly up. I should have gone through my initiation to become a made man of the family at sixteen. That was two years ago. I was granted a reprieve from the blood play because I had graduated high school early and Don Bosco thought I'd better serve the family getting my college degree first.

I've always had a knack for computers. While other kids were playing in sandboxes, I was learning to code. With technology playing an ever more important role in the business we do, Don was only too happy to encourage my talents. My father, Ricco, is his Underboss, and my brother, Luca, is in training to someday take his place. Being blood, I am predestined to someday join them in the inner circle. Having someone in that highly selective group with the computer skills I have will be a huge advantage. At least that's what Don Bosco told me.

Now, at eighteen, I have my college degree. I could ask for more time to get my master's but, not to sound cocky, I don't need it. Reading and writing code comes as easy as reading a book. I know I have more to learn. I just won't be learning it in a classroom.

The date hasn't been set. It's coming soon. I'm ready for it. Or at least I will be after this weekend. I have one last loose end to tie up. My girl. I need to come clean to her about who I am. Who my family is.

Who THE family is.

So far, I've been able to shield her from the darker side of my life. We had agreed to keep our relationship on the down-low until graduation. For her, it was to allow her to keep her focus on her studies. For me, it was so I could keep her hidden from my family. Not that I don't love my family. I do. It's the secrets that I'm worried about. The enemies that will seek to hurt her for her association with me.

I wish I could keep her all to myself a little longer. Forever if possible.

It's not. That's not the life of a mafia man. If we are to have a future, I need to tell her about the family.

She wasn't born into my world. Her parents were both doctors before they died in a car accident five years ago. My girl's been alone ever since. Well, until I found her.

We met by chance a year ago when we bumped into each other at our mutual advisor's office. We bonded over the fact we were both early high school graduates and the youngest kids on campus.

I was so impressed with her, not only did she graduate high school early and was taking college courses already, she was going through the courts to get herself emancipated and out of foster care. She was always an independent spirit, and her parent's had a healthy inheritance left for her, so the transition was fairly smooth. Better than living in a crowded foster home where she didn't even get her own bedroom. I knew then that I needed her in my life.

She is amazing. Brilliant. Smarter than me, and I have no problem admitting it. She's sixteen, nearly seventeen, and just graduated alongside me. Only where I went for computer science, she went pre-med. Now she's on to Medical School. Following in her parent's footsteps just like she promised at their funeral.

I've been given permission from the Don to tell her about me. About the family. I've hated having to hide so much of my life from her, and I know that in order for us to build a future together, I need her to know the real me. Know the family she will someday be a part of. After this weekend, she will have my protection too. The protection of the Caruso name.

Tonight I'm taking her to my family's lake house. We'll have the place to ourselves until Sunday when my family will join us for dinner. I know my girl is nervous. She thinks my parents are rich entrepreneurs with their hands in various investments throughout the city. I don't like lying to her, so I told a partial truth. The Caruso family does have investments, and businesses all over the city.

"Tino, how formal is dinner going to be on Sunday?" She asks. I love that she calls me Tino. Everyone else calls me Val or Valentino. She wanted something special, something only she would call me.

I had been so wrapped up in my thoughts, I forgot I was supposed to be helping her pack for the weekend. I move from where I was leaned against the doorway, to join her at the closet.

"Only semi. Dad and Luca will be in suits but probably no tie. I'll be in slacks and a button up." I reply. Men in the family always wear suits. I hate them. I prefer jeans and sweatshirts. Grabbing her around the waist I pull her back to my front. Her whole body melts into me. She fits perfectly in my arms. Her gorgeous brown hair hangs long down her back in soft waves that tickle my cheek as I tuck my face into her neck. There isn't a drop of make-up on her heart shaped face. Her skin is clear and dewy. Emerald eyes emphasized by long dark lashes. She's the most beautiful woman in the world, and she's mine.

She spins so she can wrap her arms around me. Her chin rests against my chest while her head is angled up so I can see her face. "And your mom?"

I give her a quick peck on the nose. I have to stop myself from doing more. Waiting has been torturous, but I respected her decision. This weekend will be our first time and I'm beyond fucking thrilled to finally get my girl into bed. I silently reprimand myself. Focus. Dress. Looking up over her head, I quickly scan through the items still hanging on the rack and not littered on the bed or floor.

Finding the one I want, I grab it and pull it out. It's a knee length, navy blue tea dress. I've seen her wear it once before. Our first date. It hugs her curves just enough to show off her hourglass shape, which I love. The blue is a power color which dad and Luca will notice and respect. And the design is similar to the ones my mother favors. "Mom loves to dress up. Wear this and she'll be dragging you out shopping every weekend with her."

Having gone the last few years without a mother figure, I know my girl is missing out, and hoping my mother will take a liking to her. I want to instill confidence in my girl. Honestly though, my mother would drag her shopping with her no matter what she wears to dinner. Mom always wanted a little girl to spoil. Soon she will. Then both my favorite girls will have what they desire.

She takes the dress from my hands with a smile. Without

question she tucks it into her suitcase. Returning to the closet, she grabs shoes to match. I watch her continue to grab things from various places around the room and bathroom. The smile never leaves my face. I love watching her move around. She doesn't add any sway to her hips and yet my eyes never leave her. I should probably feel like a creep for staring. I don't. She's mine.

The buzzing of my phone forces me to drag my eyes away from her. It's a text from Santo. He's the Don's Uncle and adviser. "It's time."

Fuck. No, no, no. Everyone knows I was spending the weekend with my girl. Shit. You don't say no to an order. Especially not your initiation summons. I scrub my hand through my hair. We're supposed to be leaving within the hour.

"Hey babe?" I try to keep my voice calm. Inside I'm raging. I don't want to disappoint my girl.

She pokes her head into the room. "Yeah?" Her voice is light and cheery, same with the smile on her lips. Until she sees my face. A frown instantly forms. "What is it Tino? Everything okay?" She walks into the room and over to me. I'm sitting on the edge of her bed. Taking hold of her hips, I grab the belt loops on her jeans and pull her close. I duck my head and place it on her stomach. Her hands instantly begin massaging my scalp.

Taking a deep breathe, and holding it. I give myself a moment before I reply. "Something's come up. Family stuff. I have to head out." It's a terrible excuse. I won't lie to her, but I don't have time to explain everything. I can feel her breath pause in her lungs. Standing, I take her face in my hands. Making sure to look directly in her eyes. "I'm not canceling. This weekend means too much to me. To us. I'll be there. I promise. I'm just going to be a couples hours late."

Exhaling the breath she was holding, she gives a nod. Or at least tries to. My hands holding her cheeks make it difficult. She's dealt with my last minute excuses before. I hate it, but love that she's understanding. It bodes well for our future together. There will undoubtedly be many more situations that I'll need to be off in a rush without being able to tell her what I'm doing, only that it's family business. "Should we just wait until morning to go?" She asks. It's already four in the afternoon. Truth is, I don't know how long I'll be. I can only hope it doesn't take all night.

I pull her in tighter to me and kiss her. It will only make it harder to leave, but I need her to feel how much I want to stay. I pull back after her mouth has been thoroughly ravished. Her cheeks are pink and she's breathing heavier. We both are. I nip her lips once more. Unable to help myself. "Why don't you head up now? Get settled in. Explore the house. Relax in the hot tub."

"You sure?"

Kissing her one last time before pulling away. "Absolutely." Taking the key to the house from my pocket, I tuck it into her pocket for her. "I'll be there as soon as I can, and I won't be leaving your side the entire weekend."

"I'm holding you to that promise."

"Scouts honor."

"You weren't a scout." She teases.

A laugh bursts from my chest. "Okay, fine. How about pinky promise?" I stick my pinky up.

She wraps her tiny finger around mine and repeats. "Pinky promise."

"No take backs." I say.

This time she's the one who laughs. "No take backs." She agrees.

I lean in close and whisper in her ear. "Hope you realize

you just agreed to do everything with me, including shower." I kiss her cheek and slowly walk backwards away. "Naked."

Shaking her head, she continues to laugh. "Counting on it."

I mock surprise and slap a hand to my chest. "Dirty girl!"

"Yours." Her teasing tone is gone. She's all business. My serious girl.

"Damn right!" I give her one last look and blow a kiss. If the guys in the family ever saw me blow a kiss I'm sure they'd give me endless shit for it. I wouldn't care. It would be worth it. "I've really got to go. I'll see you soon babe." The L word nearly slipped out. We haven't said it yet. It's been on the tip of my tongue for a while. I do love her. With every fiber of my being. Every piece of my soul. I've been waiting for the right time.

As much as leaving my girl sucks, I admit, I'm excited to finally join the ranks of made men in my family. It's been a long time coming. It's what I've trained for.

Fifteen minutes later I'm pulling into the compound. My heart is pounding in my chest. It's not nerves. Not exactly. It's hard to explain. I've known for over a decade I would be expected to kill. To take life when needed for the family. Now that the time is here, my body is preparing itself. Adrenaline is beginning to course through my veins as I make my way to the Don's office.

There is no need to knock. The doors are open. Stepping inside, I am surprised at the number of men in the room. Usually the initiation is done by your direct report and the Capo of your region. I'm a son of the Underboss so I technically report to him. My father is standing beside Don Bosco in front of his desk. Santo stands slightly behind them, leaning against the window sill. My brother, Luca, is standing by the wall of bookshelves. His presence surprises me, as does Massimo's. He's in the corner, standing like a silent sentry. He's Luca's best friend, and like another brother to me. We've all grownup together.

Don is the first to greet me. "Valentino, my boy! How are you?"

I make sure to take his offered hand and shake it firmly. It's the first test. "I'm well sir. And you?" Using my hand he pulls me in for a hug.

"Always so damn formal." He ruffles my hair like he did when I was a boy. I suppose in his eyes I still am. You aren't a man in the family until you're a made man. "Before we get to the main event, let's sit." He says as he gestures to the couches.

Don and Luca take a seat on one side of the room, my father and I on the other. Massimo and Santo remain where they are.

"What I am about to say does not leave this room. Understood?"

I nod. "Of course sir."

"Good." He leans forward. His arms resting on his knees. "Without a male heir of my own, I have decided to arrange a marriage for my daughter. The council has agreed that her husband of my choosing will become my successor." I don't interrupt, but nod along so he knows I am listening and understand. The line of succession in our family must follow blood or get approval from the council, failure to do so has resulted in a bloody and deadly civil war in the past. No one wants a repeat of that. "In ten years' time, the man to marry my daughter, will be your brother. Luca."

Holy shit!

Talk about dropping a bomb. I try not to let my shock show on my face. I'm not sure how successful I am. I'm honestly too stunned to care. Turning to Luca, his face is his

8

usual stoic, firm, expressionless face. Only the twinkle in his eye gives away his excitement. Even knowing Luca was meant to be Underboss which is only a step below Boss, neither of us believed there was ever a chance he would get to take the role. Hell, our family wasn't meant to be Underboss either. Our father wasn't anywhere on Don Bosco's radar until the night he saved his life, he was just a lowly soldier back then.

Don Bosco had been jumped in an alley. He was getting his ass beat until our father jumped in to defend him. Don immediately took a liking to Dad. They became friends, and as time went on, dad became one of his most trusted men. When Don was forced to replace his Underboss, he refused to accept anyone the Council nominated. Told them it was Dad or no one.

Don relaxes back into his seat. A smirk on his face. He turns momentarily to Luca and gives him a nod. "Val, brother. You have always had my back. The spot as Underboss should be yours." It should. But I've never wanted it. The Underboss is an enforcer role. While I'm prepared to take life, and extract information when needed, it's not a job I've ever dreamed of, even with knowing I was technically second in line for the position. Luca leans forward, similarly to the way the Don was sitting. "I'd rather you be my Consigliere."

"What?" The word slips out before I can stop it. While Underboss is the right hand man, the Consigliere is the left. It's a position that's nearly invisible to the outside world. He is the adviser, the strategist. He has the ear of the Don more than anyone else.

Luca smiles. Clearly pleased that he surprised me. "I want you by my side. There's no one I trust more. Well, except Mass." I look to the corner. Massimo gives a nod. It's a subtle gesture but tells me everything I need to know.

"Congratulations Mass." I say with a nod back.

Suddenly Don and dad start laughing. My eyes flick between them. Trying to understand the reasoning. Dad slaps a hand on my shoulder. "That is exactly why you will make a great Consigliere. You knew exactly what Luca's intentions were without needing to say them."

"Of course. With my hacking, I would be best utilized behind a desk. Massimo is literally built to be an Underboss." I reply. Then I rise and move so I stand before my brother. I place my hand over my heart. A deep sign of respect in our world. "I would be honored to be your Consigliere."

Luca stands and wraps me in a hug. We aren't big on affection. Especially in front of men of the family. "I love you bro." He whispers in my ear.

"Love you too." I whisper back with two slaps to his back.

The Don rises and claps his hands together. "Now that that is settled, let's move on to the fun part." He looks to me and gives me a wink.

We head to the basement in silence. I'm thankful for the quiet because my head is buzzing. Consigliere. It's hard to wrap my mind around. I am honored. Deeply.

I can't wait to tell my girl. She won't understand its importance. Not at first. For me, it's everything. Not just the job, the protection. As Consigliere, we will live within the walls of the compound. I will have guards and security at my disposal to watch over her. She will never be without protection. It has been my greatest fear about bringing her into my world.

The hallway through the basement is dark. There are two sides to the basement. You can't access one side from the other. The other side holds our weapons room, infirmary, and gym. This side is for our seedier business. It's soundproof and only accessible by a select few.

I walk past a few empty cells. We don't keep men in these cages long. Once they give us the information we need, they are disposed of. We enter the room at the end of the hall. I recognize the man strapped to the chair. He works at one of our clubs as a bouncer. He's an employee not family. Still we expect loyalty to any who receive a paycheck with our insignia on it.

It's customary in our family that first blood is a rite of passage. It is also not a quick kill. There is no bullet to the head or knife to the throat. It is a slow and grueling process where you showcase your skills and prove your loyalty to the family. You are not allowed to ask what they did to deserve the torture. Hell, you don't even get told if they do deserve it. It's a test of loyalty as much as anything else.

I've already been gone for hours from my girl. As I take off my suit jacket and lay it on the empty table, I shoot her a quick text letting her know I'm going to be later than expected, and to not wait up for me. I turn my phone on silent, knowing I can't be distracted. There is no clock in the room. No way to tell the passing of time. The man in the chair needs to have my undivided attention.

Next I move to the only other table in the room. An array of tools and weapons take up every inch. I'm trained to know how to use them all. Everything from the knife, to the hatchet. The sledgehammer to the blow torch. That last one being my least favorite. The smell of burning flesh does not easily vacate your nose even after you leave the room.

I start with the pliers. Learning from the best, I know I should start with things that hurt without losing a lot of blood. That will come later.

At some point Santo excuses himself from the room,

taking a phone call. Don, dad, Luca, and Massimo stay to witness as I methodically pick my victim apart. His screams echoing off the bricks.

By the time I am finished, and the Don gives me the nod of his approval, it is the early hours of the morning. I'm itching to rush to the lake house. I need my girl. The experience of taking a life was so much more than I could have imagined. I knew I could physically do it. Mentally I prepared myself as much as I could.

I was in no way prepared. My mind hadn't reacted the way I thought it would. It was like there was a beast inside me, and with every drop of blood I spilled, and every scream it heard, it grew hungrier. Wanting more. Needing more.

Even now, with the man dead, and myself washed of any remnants of the event, I can feel the beast lingering under my skin. It wants out.

I need the peace I feel with my girl. Her presence, her scent, it calms me. It's like her soul sings a lullaby only mine can hear.

 Stepping out of the house into the early morning air, I dial my girl's phone. She doesn't answer so I leave a message. She probably won't listen to it before I get there, but I leave it anyway. I tell her I'm sorry again and that I'm on my way. Once I hang up, I go to my messages. She never responded. The hairs on my arm instantly spring up and a cold chill washed over me. I sent the message at 6:15pm. There is no way she wouldn't have seen the message by now. And my girl always responds. Always.

"No. No. No…." Knowing something is wrong, I run to my car and speed like the hounds of hell are nipping at my ass all the way to the lake house. My mind running every horrible scenario over and over in my head.

Would I find her body?

A trail of blood?

A note from an enemy telling me she's been taken?

When I get into the driveway, her car isn't there. A familiar black sedan is. Santo's. He steps out of the house, just as I'm getting out of the car. There is a slip of paper in his hands. He passes it to me, as he gives my shoulder a squeeze. It's a move my father has done a thousand times. Only there is no comfort in his touch. "I'm sorry." He says. That's it. Two words. Then he is gone.

I don't look at the note right away. I know the moment I do, my life will never be the same. Hell it was never going to be the same once I stepped into the basement last night.

I move through the house and out onto the back deck. It's peaceful. Quiet. Only sound I hear is the gentle slapping of the waves against the rocky beach. I try to soak in the peaceful feeling, knowing it may be the last time I feel it.

I smooth out the crumpled paper in my hand. I recognize her handwriting even with the words hard to make out. The letters are shaky at best, like she was rushing to put the words down and be done.

Done.

That's what the letter says.

We're done.

She says she knows. She knows about the kind of man I am. And she cannot be with someone like me. She doesn't feel safe with me.

I swear my heart stops beating.

She ends the letter asking me not to contact her.

Not going after her will forever be my biggest regret.

CHAPTER TWO

Present Day - Keira

The locker-room echoes with the chants of the crowd beyond the closed doors. It's fight night in the underground world. Bets will be placed and blood will be spilled. My body thrums with excitement. The adrenaline. The pain. Both as familiar as breathing.

Killian, my friend, mentor, and fiancé, kneels in front of me. Wrapping my knuckles as he has done countless times before. He doesn't like that I fight. Doesn't like that he can't protect me while I'm in the ring. Still, every time we come, he is the one taping my hands, wiping away my blood, and icing the bruises.

I stare down at his handsome face. He means the world to me. He is my world. The only thing I have left.

I'm broken. He knows it, I know it, though we rarely talk about it. Six years ago I was in the right place at the right time. He had been beaten, shot, and left to die on the side of the road. I found him, brought him home, cleaned him up and tended to his injuries. He gave me his card, told me to call if I ever needed anything. Said he owed me a blood debt.

Two weeks later I reached out to him and cashed it in.

The door opens. Without looking, I know it's just Grady. He's Killian's best friend and business partner. He's also the only man ballsy enough to enter this room without knocking.

"Crowd is double what it was last Saturday. You ready for this Cahira?" He asks as he strolls closer.

I don't even need to think about it. "Always." I didn't fight last Saturday. Crowds are always larger on nights I fight. While female fighters are becoming more common, female fighters that willingly fight the men are rare. Female fighters that beat those men were unheard of. At least until I entered the ring sixteen months ago. Forty-eight fights and I am still undefeated.

Killian stands. I follow suit. He leans his forehead against mine. "Forty-nine. He's got a hundred pounds on you. All his strength is in his arms. Bring him to his knees and you've got him."

I knock my knuckles against his. "That's why you don't skip leg day."

Both men give a snort. I like surprising them with jokes. They used to tell me I was too serious. I agree. I wasn't always. There was a time when I smiled without thought, laughed freely, joked, teased, and flirted. Fighting has brought my confidence back. It's given me physical as well as mental strength. It also gives me something to focus on when the noise in my head becomes too much. When the fear and doubt threaten to overwhelm me.

I step away from Killian so I can do a few bounces on my toes and shake my head to get the blood pumping. There's no room for negative thoughts tonight. Focus.

Killian leads the way out of the room. I follow closely behind, with Grady at my back. Stepping into the ring, I take a moment to assess my opponent. The man is huge. A smile creeps onto my face. The bigger they are, the harder they fall. My smile hides the hint of fear that creeps in. I'm not psychotic. I don't have a death wish. I know this man could kill me with one well-placed punch.

I don't want to die. I don't go seeking it out. It's the pain I chase. My body feels lost without it. It's like I no longer notice it as it ravages my body. I only notice its absence.

Speaking of pain, I hear the loud crunch of bone moments before a sharp, searing, agony washes over my ribs. Fuck that hurt.

I was so lost in my head, I hadn't realized the fight had begun. Ducking under the next jab, I quickly get out of the corner and across the mat. It only takes a moment for my opponent to follow. Each breath brings a wave of fresh pain. It's exactly what I needed. My body releases a flow of adrenalin. I instantly feel its effects working through every cell of my body. Strumming it to life.

We attack and counter through two rounds. We are in our last. I can see his arms tiring. It's time to end this.

Jab. Jab. Cross. Uppercut. Drop to the floor and sweep the legs. The giant falls to his knees. He's nearly as tall as me in this position. Good. I do another few jabs, then roundhouse kick him.

Timber.

Eyes roll back in his head as he crashes to the mat. He's out cold.

Forty-nine.

The warehouse goes silent. It's never silent. I swear you can hear a pin drop. In the silence one voice shouts "fuck yeah". It's the voice of Grady. A moment later, he and Killian are lifting me up into their arms. Their actions break the spell on the crowd. The cheering returns ten-fold. The audience chants the name Cahira. A gift from Killian after I won my first fight. Means warrior.

We make our escape while the crowd continues to go wild. Bets are trying to be placed for my next fight, which isn't even scheduled yet.

Killian rounds on me the moment the door is closed behind us. "What the fuck was that Cahira?" His hands are on my tank top, ripping it off my body. He's not gentle. At least not until his eyes land on the bruise already forming on my ribs. Shit. I'm guessing two are broken, and a third is fractured. It's not the first time it's happened. But it feels like the worst. "He could have killed you. Why the fuck didn't you dodge? You're better than this."

"Easy Kill." Grady says, trying to defuse the tension. It doesn't work. Killian takes a step away from me and whips the nearest chair against the wall. Its wood and splinters apart like it was made of glass.

I get it. I do. Killian cares for me. Is protective of me. If the punch had been any harder, a rib bone could have punctured my lung, or a hit like that to the head could have meant lights out. Permanently.

"I didn't do it on purpose Killian." I say. There isn't any reasoning with him when he's like this, but still I try.

He spins around and pins me with a glare that would send grown men to their knees in submission. "Bullshit." He stalks closer to me again. Stopping when his face is inches from mine. "You have a fucking death wish. I've respected your need for secrets in the past, but I'm done." I open my mouth to retort. Before I can utter a word, he is continuing. "I want a fucking name. Someone hurt you. I'll fucking kill them. Just give me a name."

"No." I mean for it to come out sounding stronger than it did. Clearing my throat and pulling my shoulders back, I start again. "It doesn't matter Killian, it's in the past. I've moved on."

Grady surprises me by being the one to speak next. "No, you haven't. You tried to bury that shit. Don't even try to deny it. Killian and I can recognize it, cause we've done that shit too. But let me tell you, it never fucking works."

"It's working just fine for…" I was going to say me, but the word is cut off when the air freezes in my lungs. Killian has his hand pressing into my fresh bruise. The pain is blinding. Literally. I see stars swirling where his face should be.

"Like I said. Bullshit. You wanted the pain. You like the pain." He says as he pulls his hand away and replaces it with an ice pack I don't remember him grabbing.

My mind has been a mess all week. It's this time of year. It's a painful reminder of what I can never have. The pain in my ribs continues to throb. It's has a direct line to my mouth, and I snap. "Yes. I like the pain. I love the pain. It's the only thing that normally forces my mind to shut up." I slump against the wall and drop to the ground. I bring my knees up as much as my ribs allow. I want to crawl into a ball and cry. I won't. I can't. I haven't cried in years. "It's not working anymore."

Killian takes a seat to my right. Grady on my left. "You aren't alone anymore. You don't have to be scared of the shadows anymore. They can't get to you with us." I lean into Killian. Absorbing his words. They are the same ones he said to me when the nightmares used to wake me up in the dead of night, screaming.

"It's not the shadows that still plague me. I know you'll keep me safe from them. It's the what-ifs. There is a constant stream of scenarios running through my head. Every variable of how my life might have been."

"You never got closure." Adds Grady. Understanding swims in his eyes.

I shake my head. No. I never did. There was a lot of things I never got.

Things that went unsaid.

CHAPTER THREE
Val

Sitting at my computer in the corner of the Don's office, I'm only partially listened to Massimo in the background grumbling about the female prisoner in the basement. The family has a strict no women or children are to be harmed policy.

Unfortunately the sentiment wasn't unanimously accepted among the ranks. In fact, the worst offender had been Santo. That bastard. We only recently learned of his deception. It seems every day we are discovering new ways he fucked with all of our lives. Controlling us like a puppet master, and we were completely oblivious.

I'm glad he's dead. In fact, I want to bring him back to life just to kill him again. The asshole had been manipulating and double crossing us. He was stealing from the family. Using our territory as a hunting ground for the Cartel's human trafficking ring.

His betrayal goes back decades. Twenty years ago he even ran the Don's high school sweetheart, Violet, out of the city while she was unknowingly pregnant.

Once Santo had learned of the baby, he sent men after them both. He knew the child had claim to the throne. If the council ever found out, his plans would have been ruined. Funny enough, they were ruined by the very child he tried and failed to murder. Repeatedly.

It turns out the child was a girl. Elena. The Don only found out about her when she broke into the compound and snuck into his office. She hadn't tripped a single alarm. Crazy woman had drawn a gun on her own father. Right before she kicked Luca's ass. Well, nuts actually.

Her arrival and the Intel she brought with her set off a shit storm of problems. A necessary shit storm. Turns out she is even better with computers than me, and had a whole hard-drive full of evidence on Santo, as well as a handful of rats in our ranks. Men who only claimed to be loyal, but turned on us for a couple of zeros in their bank account.

We eliminated Santo, and as many of the rats as we could find. We know there are a few we've missed or have gone underground. It's why Massimo kidnapped the woman in the basement. She's been spotted all over town with our enemies. Many of whom have turned up dead days later. She's either a black widow, or she's working for someone. Until we know who, and if she's a threat to us, Massimo will be keeping her.

With the return of Violet, and the discovery of Elena, the marriage contract Luca had with Milan was dissolved. Luca needed to marry the first-born daughter in order to take the throne. Elena wasn't thrilled about the idea. She didn't want to settle down. She had been on the run her entire life. The thought of staying in one place scared her. It's why Luca keeps a pair of handcuffs in his pocket. She's run once on him already. With the wedding tomorrow, he's even more on edge.

"Let me take a crack at her." Pipes in Elena.

Immediately Luca is on his feet. "No." You can see his hand itching to grab his handcuffs.

"Why not? It makes sense. Massimo doesn't want to hurt a woman. I'm a woman. I don't mind hitting one."

Luca scrubs a hand down his face. He's trying hard not to smother Elena. It's amusing to me. For seven years he had assumed he would marry Milan. A woman twelve years younger than him, who he doubted he would ever love. Then Elena popped up out of nowhere and sent him to his knees. Literally and metaphorically. He was smitten the moment she kicked his ass. Every instinct he has is riding him to shield her from the unscrupulous side of the family. Which is ironic, because she was the one who shot Santo first, and she's probably got a higher body count than Luca does.

She wasn't raised in the life, but she was trained for it. Ronan, a shadow mercenary, came to her mother's aid on the side of the road, while she was in labor. He helped deliver Elena and has been her unofficial godfather ever since. Over the years he's trained her in everything from self-defense, lock picking, weapons, computer hacking, and interrogation.

"Because I don't want you in the basement." Elena opens her mouth to interrupt. Luca stops her with a hand over her mouth. "I know you can handle it. I'm not doubting your skills." He removes his hand and replaces it with his lips.

I turn in my seat to go back to my work. I'm happy for my brother. He deserves happiness. He deserves love.

I don't.

Ever since Santo's betrayals came to light, I've been plagued with doubts of the past. Doubts about the day at the lake house. Why was Santo there? I never questioned it at the time. I was too distraught. I had planned to only give my girl a few days to cool down, then I was going to find her and force her to talk to me.

I never did go to her. Santo kept me busy. Every day he was giving me a new lead to track, a new man to take out. I was vicious, hungry. The beast in me had been unleashed and I didn't have my girl to calm me. The rage from her leaving me festered. By the time the red faded from my vision, months had gone by. She had remained radio silent. Her apartment was cleared out, and she had taken leave from school. Looking back, I should have saw it as the sign it was.

There was no way my girl would have quit med school. It was her dream. A promise to her parents that she made after they died.

Did Santo say something to my girl? Did he threaten her? Did he hurt her? I don't even know if she's alive. There is no online activity or records of her in six years. I've been trying to track her down in every spare moment I have. The family's rat problem has been coming first. Or it should. It's getting harder and harder to keep my mind on task. There is a soul deep ache within me. The blood hungry beast I buried in the past wants answers.

Fuck it.

Elena can look into our problem. I need to find my girl. My Keira.

No, not my girl. Not anymore.

Could she be again? It's been seven years. Maybe she's married. Does she have kids and a white picket fence? Did she end up becoming a doctor?

Is she buried in an unmarked grave, or was she tossed into the lake?

Before I realize it, my fists are slamming against the table. "Everything alright Val?" Asks Massimo.

"No." I close my laptop and rip the power cord from the wall. "No. Nothing is fucking alright. I need to fucking find her." I say as I storm out of the room.

CHAPTER FOUR

Keira

I tug at the bottom of my dress. Trying to get it down as far as it can go. It's not exactly short. Everything is covered. It ends mid-thigh, and only rides up slightly when I walk.

"Relax." Killian whispers into my ear. "You look perfect. They're going to love you."

"Couldn't they love me while I was wearing pants?" I retort. Damn, I miss my leggings and scrubs. Killian laughs and brings my knuckles to his lips. I wait for the butterflies to flutter. Nothing. They are as dead as my heart. It makes me angry for Killian. He asked me to marry him knowing I would never love him. I don't even lust for him. He's a good looking guy. Muscular, chiseled jaw, and an ass you can bounce a quarter off of. I should be thrilled to marry him. I'm not. It's a business arrangement.

He needed a wife that he can trust. Someone who will help him to keep the secret he guards. And I needed protection. A name and money I could hide behind. Killian had given me both years ago. A new identity and an impenetrable fortress to live in. There were no strings attached to it. Yet when he asked me to agree to marry him, I didn't hesitate. He wasn't looking for love. Secrets were more important to keep. People were safer that way.

"You know my family is old fashion." He replies with a grin.

It makes me want to punch him in his pretty face. "Yes. Yes." I grumble before repeating the rules I must follow. "Women can't wear pants at family functions. Heels need to be at least three inches. Hair freshly done, and make-up caked in ridiculous layers. God forbid someone sees I have freckles. Oh, and I am to defer to you in all decisions that may arise throughout the night." I nudge my shoulder into him as the car pulls to a stop. "Kind of fucked up of you to choose the undefeated underground MMA fighter slash surgeon to marry." He laughs.

"It's about time my family had a shake up." Killian says as the driver knocks on the window. Killian knocks back. The door is opened and he steps out, then offers his hand to me. It's a struggle to keep myself covered while maneuvering, but I somehow manage. Once I'm steady on my feet. Killian leans in to whisper. "My cousins have become too complacent with my father's reign. Or lack thereof. Tonight we take the first step to taking over the family business."

Stepping back, he takes my hand and tucks it into the crook of his arm. We're at the marina, heading to a massive yacht. It's larger than any boat I've ever seen. I should have expected it. Killian's family is insanely rich.

Once boarded, we are handed glasses of champagne. I pretend to sip mine. We need to remain clear headed tonight. "You going to be okay for a bit?" Killian asks.

"Yeah, go get 'em boss man." I tease. Killian gives me a chaste kiss on the cheek before wandering off to find his father.

I make slow loops around the boat. With nothing in common with these people, I don't join into conversation. I people watch. The men speak of money and business I know nothing about.

The woman are equally as unimpressive to commune with. They throw false compliments at each other and laugh loud and high pitched as though they just heard the greatest joke in the world.

Nothing is that funny.

Fake.

They are all fake.

Well I suppose I do have that in common with them. I'm here to play the doting, loving fiancé. The sweet, regal, docile, arm candy. I am anything but that.

Damn, I wish I could have a drink. I make my way to the bar, dodging a few "accidental" ass grabs. They are lucky I'm quick on my feet. If one of them had succeeded in touching me, I would have had their ass on the floor, and their testicles stabbed by my stiletto. Huh, I hadn't thought of them as a weapon. Perhaps there is a use to wearing them after all.

I order a coke from the bartender just as Grady appears out of nowhere. "Fucking ridiculous." He grumbles as he chugs back my coke like it's a shot of tequila."

The bartender is quick to replace it. "Agreed." I reply as I grab my drink before Grady can a second time. I sip it and ask. "Now what did I agree to?"

Grady asks the bartender for his own coke and gives a laugh. "The level of ass kissing. It's ridiculous." He looks over his shoulder. Then looks down and does a spin.

I try to see what he is looking at, but I don't notice anything wrong. "What are you doing?"

He does another spin, this time looking over the opposite

shoulder and spinning the other direction. "Looking at my ass."

He says it with such seriousness. It only confuses me further. "Why?" I ask before I take another sip.

"Trying to see if I have any lipstick on my ass. I just bought these pants." His statement catches me off guard, and I laugh. I laugh so hard, soda starts to come out my nose. I scramble to get a napkin. Before I can, one is placed in my hand, and an arm snags around my middle. I freeze for a moment, my muscles coil and prepare to attack. A moment later, I recognize Killian's cologne. He's is so lucky.

The smile on Grady's face and the nod at the figure behind me, further allow me to relax. Killian gives me a kiss on the neck. "Sorry my dear." He says, playing into our role as a happy couple. "My cousin wanted to discuss business."

"Everything okay?" I ask, as I spin in his arms, and bring my hands to the back of his neck. It looks like an intimate moment, when really it's an excuse to get close enough to talk without risk of someone overhearing.

"Fuck no. I got away as soon as I could." I give a laugh at his playful pout. "Did you find your father?"

"No, I think he's below deck. He should be out soon. He always likes to make a toast. You know shake hands, kiss babies." I nod in understanding.

Suddenly a commotion breaks out on the other side of the room. Killian's asshole cousin is clinking his glass. Begging for attention. "What the fuck is he doing?" Grumbles Grady. Killian goes to make a move towards his cousin. Grady stops him with a hand to the shoulder.

It takes us both a moment to realize Grady had spotted trouble before we did.

Hands behind his back, gun to his head, Killian's father is led to the cousin's side by some ugly goon. Greasy hair, ill-fitting suit. Looks like a damn drug addict getting anxious for his next hit.

"Son of a bitch." Growls Killian. Right before several more gunman appear around the room and begin to circle around the crowd. "Secure an exit." He whispers to Grady, who gives a barely noticeable nod before he's gone. Like literally disappears.

"Did you know?" I ask.

"I had a hunch." He says. I figured as much. Killian had spent far too much time in meetings the last two days for him not to have been making contingency plans for this trip.

"We ready for it?""

He gives me a wink and a smile. "Of course. Why do you think none of my men are here?"

"And yet you brought me along." I tease, knowing even though he hadn't let me in on the plan, that I had a role to play in the game. I'm not worried. I trust Killian.

"Would you have wanted to miss out on the fun?" Fucker knows I wouldn't. I would have bitched his ass out if he came home with another knife or bullet wound and I hadn't been there.

Turning my focus back to the gunmen. "Are we going to try to save your father?"

He looks to his dad. He loves his father. Knows he did his best to hold the family together after they lost Killian's mother.

From across the room, his father makes eye contact with him, then gives a small shake of his head, before squaring his shoulders, his head held high. "If I can." Killian replies with conviction.

I'm only partially listening as his cousin begins a speech about how business has been failing. "There needs to be a better leader. One who isn't afraid to take risks. One that will bring in new business. There is an opportunity for us to expand our reach. Deepen our pockets." That's when Killian's father starts to fight back. He breaks the nose of one guard, then rams his knee into the junk of another. All while working his way backwards towards the railing on the side of the ship.

The cousin doesn't acknowledge the interruption as he continues to speak. "To bring in the new, we need to remove the old." The cousin turns to Killian's dad as pulls out a gun from underneath his suit jacket. "Good-bye and good riddance old man."

Bam. The cousin fires a single shot. The dad falters back a few steps then crashes over the railing and disappears into the water with a splash. Before I can storm over to his cousin, Killian grabs my arm and begins dragging me away. Taking his queue, I pick up my pace and follow him. We're rounding the bar when more shots are fired. This time into the crowd. The door behind the bar opens and two armed men appear. Killian disarms one guard. While he takes care of one, I set my sights on the second. I grab a champagne glass from the shelf, then bash the liquid end onto the cooler so it breaks in half, leaving me with the stem that now resembles a small knife. The second guard takes one look at me and must determine I'm not much of a threat. I get it. I'm five-four compared to his six foot something. I'm wearing a tiny dress and heals. In no way do I look like a threat, let alone an undefeated underground champ.

The fool turns his back on me, to jump into the fight with Killian and the other guard. I don't let him take two steps before I'm on his back. The point of the flute stem buried in his throat. Severing his artery.

I've fought nearly a hundred men, in self-defense, in the ring, and in practice. Never have I dealt a fatal blow. Until now. I jump off his back as he falls to the floor. I can't do anything but stare. As a doctor I'm meant to do no harm.

"Well fuck that." I declare to myself. When your life is in danger by psychos with guns, you fight. You fight to get away or you fight to the death.

Grady rushes to us as Killian snaps the neck of the first man. The crunch of tendons and possible bone send a shiver down my spine. I decide I'll worry about the blood on my hands later. We've still got shit to deal with now.

"Ready for you port side, boss." Grady hollers before running, gun drawn into the chaos.

Killian approaches slowly. "You did good." He says as he takes my hand once more. We reverse directions and head back out from behind the bar. I hike the dress up over her hips. The damn thing is too tight and restrictive for this kind of physical activity. Thank god I thought to wear my bike shorts underneath.

Killian turns back to me as we sneak along the wall. The gun fire has stopped. There doesn't appear to be many dead or dying. The ceiling is littered with holes. Looks like the gunfire may have been warning or intimidation shots. "No thong. That's disappointing." He says as we stop at the edge of a group cowering against a line of sofas.

Of course he would try to make me laugh in a situation like this. "Need to keep moving." I remind him as his eyes remain locked on my shorts.

He gives a nod, and tears his eyes away from my legs. As we move further across the room, guilt threatens to overwhelm me. There are several people injured and bleeding. They need medical attention. I have to ignore every instinct in my body telling me to help them.

Killian must see the struggle in my eyes, and tugs me harder.

31

We get to the side of the boat, where the wall has turned into railing, without further incident. Killian climbs over first. As he reaches out to help me over, a single shot rings out. Blood blooms on Killian's chest as he loses his grip and falls into the water.

"No!" I scream.

Fucker.

I'm pissed. Enraged. Angry. Fucking livid. I spin to find the cousin only a few feet away. Gun still smoking. A sadistic grin on his face. He is paying no attention to me. His eyes are on the dark water.

While he is focused elsewhere, I take the opportunity to charge him. He loses his balance and we tumble to the ground. I fight to extract the gun from his grip. His eyes flick to mine. Completely confused as to what just happened. Then the smirk returns to his face.

I wipe it off with an open handed slap to the face. Stunned, his hand instantly flies up to rub it. As though he cannot believe he just got bitch slapped. "Believe it asshole." I say.

The slap must have knocked the sense back into him, because he begins to shout for his guards. "Grab her." Hands pull at my arms from behind.

This is what I've trained for.

Never again will I be weak and unable to fight back.

I'm still close enough to the cousin to reach him with my feet. He thinks he has me cowed. Idiot. One swift kick and he drops to his knees. Hands cupping his balls as he moans in pain. The hands on me loosen slightly. Enough for me to drop to the floor like dead weight.

This breaks their grip completely. On the floor, I sweep my leg in a circle. It knocks one of the guards to the ground. I jump back up to my feet, then quickly land a couple combo punch to the ribs of the second guy, before sending a final punch to his throat. He drops just like the cousin. Gasping for air.

"Cahina!" I hear screamed from somewhere below. "Move that gorgeous ass!" It's Killian. Thank god.

Looking around, I notice the cousin has run off, and everyone else is scrambling to evacuate as well. Smoke is coming from somewhere below deck.

"Damn it." I mumble to myself as I leap over the railing and into the darkness to join Killian.

CHAPTER FIVE

Keira

An hour later, my hands shake as I try to finish the stitches on Killian's shoulder. The shot went straight through. Missed everything major and didn't even hit bone. He's lucky. Another inch in any direction and it could have shattered his collarbone, or tore through an artery. A few inches and it would have hit his heart.

"Cahina." I don't answer. "Doc." Killian says as he grabs my hands. He pulls them back as Grady grabs the needle from my hand and finishes up the stitch.

I try to turn from him. To find something else to keep my hands and mind busy. I need to focus on him. Getting him on the road to recovery. If I keep busy, I can't think of the blood. Blood that isn't his or mine. That I spilled.

I'm meant to heal. It's my life's work. My parent's work.

"Doc." He says again. Louder this time.

"Almost done." I reply. I'm not. I'm not working on anything. I'm staring at my hands. His fingers come into my field of view, and cover my own. "Grady's got this. He was

34

stitching me up long before you came around. You need to sit. You need to process."

"What is there to process?" I can't look at him. Will he see me different? Am I different? "I did what I had to."

"And you saved my life by doing it. That's three times you've saved me. I'm supposed to be the one protecting you." I can hear the pain in his voice. He isn't one for getting emotional, unless it's playful or angry.

I spin towards him. Grady is finishing wrapping the bandage on the wound. Confident I won't hurt him further, I stop closer to him and bring my hands to his face. There is a bruise darkening on his jaw that I avoid. "You did protect me." He starts to shake his head. I try to keep it stiff. "Yes. You have and you are." I take a deep breath to gather my thoughts. "I don't regret killing that man. I feel a lot of things, but not regret."

Killian remains silent for a moment before saying, "I'm sorry."

"I'm not." I say quickly.

"I am. You asked me to protect you. I should have done better. If I had you wouldn't have had to take a life."

I shake my head. Unwilling to let him feel blame for tonight. If it's anyone's fault, it's his cousin's. "I told you. I don't regret it." I take a step back from him and fold my arms across my chest. Trying to mimic the stance Grady and him always take when they are trying to get me to back down on a fight. "I would do it again."

He raises an eyebrow at me. Obviously not expecting that answer, so I continue. "I've seen the evil in this world. The darkness and destruction they cause. Those men are evil. Were evil." I pause for a moment. "The things your cousin is planning…We can't let him succeed."

"I won't." Declares Killian. The steel in his voice

returning.

"We won't." I correct. "I'm in this with you. One hundred percent. Even if it means I need to kill again." As I speak the words, I realize how true they are.

"You fuckers better not leave me out. I'm in this too." Chimes Grady as he steps closer again, forming a circle with our bodies. Together we laugh.

"I need to check on your father." I say as I look over to the makeshift hospital bed behind me. He took a shot to the chest too, only his was lower and did internal damage to his organs. He's alive, but unconscious. I needed to induce a coma. As long as he doesn't succumb to infection, he will live. He was smart to move to the rail, so he could fall over it. Whether intentional or not, it probably saved his life. A second shot to the chest would have killed him. At least now he has a chance.

"I need to call a meeting." Killian says as Grady helps him to pull on a clean shirt.

I give a nod. "I'll stay and watch over him." I say as I motion to his dad. Killian kisses my temple before leaving with Grady, who gives me a hug before he follows.

CHAPTER SIX

Val

Club Vivid is crowded, as usual. I hate it here. It's too loud, and there are too many drunk people grinding on each other. There was a time I had tried to be like them. To join them in their debauchery.

For months I spent every weekend trying to loose myself in alcohol. The women never appealed to me. Not like they did to Luca and Massimo. Those two had a new woman in bed every week.

I had tried. I thought it would get my mind off of Keira. Help me to move on. It didn't. Every woman who came onto me, I danced with, or gave me their number, I compared to Keira. I wasn't fortunate enough to find someone who came close, so I stopped looking. I figured the first woman I'd have would end up being whoever Don Bosco arranged for me to marry. If I fell in love with her, great. If I didn't, I'd find a way to satisfy her and have an heir or two. I had lived this long without sex. I could go a little longer.

Except now that Bosco had Violet again, Luca captured

37

Elena, and Massimo turned our innocent prisoner from the basement, Livianna, into an obsession, I was surrounded by love and happiness. I was thrilled for them. But it led to me spending more time thinking about Keira. I don't want to believe she's dead. Instead I wonder where she is, or what she is doing.

I have a lead. Just the one. It's not a strong one, and I'm itching to return home to chase it further. I found a name, a doctor whose history before six years ago is sketchy at best. It seems someone created her identity around the same time Keira's cuts off. Soon, I hope to have more time to pursue the lead.

Elena and I have been busy combing over camera footage from all over the city. Our last rat in the family, Joseph, is still out there. He hasn't been seen, but we know he hasn't left the city. I've got alerts set up at every plane, train, and bus station. Every cop on our payroll has his picture, and Elena set up a program to scan every face that passes by a traffic camera either on foot or in a vehicle to scan facial rec for a match. We've flagged his credit cards and bank accounts as well, so if he tries to access them, we'll know.

Because we've been working so hard, the girls convinced Luca and Massimo to take them out tonight. I'm here to help keep an eye on the girls, as well as play lookout for Joseph or anyone from the Cartel. We took out one of their local leaders Julio, and captured the other, Ramirez, but that fucker escaped. It's only a matter of time before he screws up and we catch him again. This time, he won't be able to escape. If Luca or Massimo don't kill him, I will.

I spot Massimo and Livianna descending the stairs from his office moments before my phone goes off. Strange. It's a text from Massimo. "Cartel's here. They're hunting. Livianna's taking lead. Don't move in until I say."

Well damn. I turn to find Luca and Elena. They have stopped dancing and are making their way over to me. Not a minute later and we've got the signal from Massimo. They're on the move. Now, so are we. Our SUVs are out back. We quickly divide ourselves among them and start chasing. It's not an exciting car chase. We play a shell game to keep them from catching on to being followed. We only have one car following a few cars behind at a time, and every few blocks we switch out with a new car following while the others trail a block away. We are in constant communication with each other, so we don't lose them.

They lead us to the shipyard. The women are told to stay in the car. Elena only does so after Luca threatens her. I'm doubtful she'll stay behind for long. Livianna agrees to stay in the car only after Massimo practically begs her. She's a sucker for his begging and he knows it.

We enter the building through multiple doors. It's a good thing we did because there are more men here than we predicted. Bullets begin to fly. Wood shavings spatter into the air as the crate I dove behind gets obliterated by bullets. I return fire and keep moving. I make my way around the room to get behind the men. We didn't have time to properly surround them before our entry and I can see several making their escape through the far door.

Massimo and Luca reach it first and take off outside. Al, Luca's bodyguard and driver is hot on my tail. There are a few last gunshots before I hear Massimo scream. "NO!"

Fuck. There is a car that's been t-boned. It takes me a moment to realize that it's one of our cars. The one Livianna promised to stay in. The four of us are running to get to her as quickly as we can. Massimo has us all beat. He gets to the cars as the driver of the other vehicle gets out and is ripping Livianna's door open. She is slumped against the wheel, and I can see blood running down her forehead.

The bastard rips her from the car, and hits her over the head, just before Massimo tackles him to the ground. He doesn't stop there. He rains hellfire down on the man. His face isn't even recognizable as a face by the time Luca stops him. "Mass enough. He's dead." Massimo's fist pauses mid-air. "Liv needs you."

Like coming out of a trance, Massimo's attention snaps back to Livianna. "I'm so sorry sweetheart." He's rocking her in his arms. One of our men was a field medic in the army, he's quick to get to their side and start evaluating her.

I return to the building. The woman who was kidnapped, and that we followed here, is being led out of the building by one of our men. Fifteen more follow. They all look like shit. No offense to them. I'm sure they have been through hell. I just pray the Cartel didn't have time to do more than lock them up. Even if they didn't, they will feel the full and unrelenting wrath of the Caruso Mafia.

Our men lead them to the SUVs as more of our back-up arrives. They bring water and blankets. I take over helping the latest victim. She still has the drugs in her system and is unsteady on her feet.

A series of screeching tires has me tensing and pushing the woman behind me and pulling out my gun again.

"Where is she?" Barks a man in a suit as he exits the third vehicle to come skidding to a stop.

Luca approaches him with Elena at his side, her gun pointed at the man in the suit, while Luca's is in his hand at his side. "Who are you?" He asks.

The man in the suit stops walking. His eyes scan the carnage littering the parking lot. He smiles. The crazy ass smiles. He must be mafia. Russian if I had to guess. "Looks like you had a hell of a party." He says as he takes a step closer to the nearest body. He gives it a kick with his foot so the body rolls onto its back. "Cartel?" he asks, looking back at Luca.

"Yeah." He replies. "And you are?"

The man continues to walking until he is a few feet from Luca, and extends an arm. "Ivan. Ivan Vasiliev."

Russian. I knew it. The girl behind me begins to tremble. Her blue dress is torn, and doesn't cover much skin. I take off my suit jacket and wrap it around her. I keep my arm on her back so she doesn't fall. With my other hand, I raise the bottle of water up to her lips. She jumps as the Russian starts barking again. "Lena!"

I turn to find his eyes filled with rage as he glares at me and the girl. Great, now he's coming over here. I don't cower away, or release the girl. I don't give a shit who she is to him. She can't stand on her own. He must finally realize there's something wrong with her, because he slows his pace as he nears. His eyes lose the fire towards me, as he gives me a nod of what I can only assume is appreciation. Then he takes her into his arms and carries her over to his SUV. His tone has lost some bite as he scolds her. "Viktor was fucking worried sick about you. Don't you ever pull this shit again. You hear me?"

With the rest of the girls being split amongst the vehicles, some even going with the Russians, I make my way over to Luca and Massimo. Ivan joins us a moment later.

They continue to talk. I'm not listening. My mind is elsewhere. Wondering if the future these women were saved from was the reality my Keira lived through. When Luca mentions my name then turns to me, I have no idea what they are talking about. So, I gave a noncommittal shrug in the hopes I didn't need a verbal answer to whatever he is talking about. He seems content with my response, so I go back to

41

my thoughts about Keira.

The night seems to never end. We brought all the women who needed medical attention to the hospital, and from their coordinated getting them home, or getting them to a safe house. Livianna ended up needing a few stitches, and being monitored overnight, so Luca and I stayed with them.

We're back at the Compound, and I'm exhausted. I can't wait to shower and crawl into bed. I literally drag my legs up the front stairs and into the foyer. Luca is a few steps ahead of me. "Before you go to bed, I need to speak with you and Milan."

Since you don't tell the Don no. I follow silently behind him.

Milan is already waiting in his office. "I heard about the girls. Are they okay? Do they need anything?"

Luca pulls Milan in for a hug. It's still weird as shit seeing him be affectionate towards her. For seven years he thought he was going to marry her, and he hated every moment of it. He found her annoying, conceited, and slutty. After Elena's existence was discovered, Milan's mother Ravinia threw a fit. Turns out Milan wasn't Bosco's biological daughter as they had both believed.

The contract between them was voided. Ravinia was sent to Italy. Once she was gone, the true Milan started to peak out. Turns out, she had been groomed and controlled by her mother. She hated and was looking for a way away from her. That's why she latched onto Luca. She thought he was going to save her. He didn't have to. Bosco did, while getting rid of her mother's influence and claiming her as his second daughter. DNA be damned.

The real Milan is a fucking delight. Turns out she's smart and funny. She hates make-up and heels. And she's not nearly as obsessed with Luca as we thought. Nearly every

42

interaction they had over the years was orchestrated by her mother.

When Luca pulls back from the hug, I take his place, for a hug of my own, before we all sit down. Luca's not big on the pageantry when it's those close to him, so instead of taking the seat behind his desk, he leads us to the couches.

"Milan, normally due to your age, I would not include you in discussions related to potential alliances and contracts, but as this directly involved you, I wish to get your opinion."

She sits up straighter. Clearly intrigued by the conversation. "Okay."

"There has been an offer made to form an alliance with the Russians. A man named Ivan plans to overthrow Mishkin." Milan nods along. "An alliance of this caliber would require a marriage bond. It would need to be with someone of high rank. We have two options. Val and you."

Fuck me. That's why he looked at me when he was talking to Ivan. Shit.

"Me?" Milan questions. Clearly stunned.

"Yes. As the Don's second daughter, you are technically higher ranking than Val."

"But I'm not blood." She whispers.

"Milan." Luca says scooting closer to her so he can grab her hand. "We meant it when we said you are family. To Bosco you are his daughter. Same as Mario. To the rest of us, you are our sister, by law or by choice."

"I thought you were just being polite. Like giving me the safety and housing of a daughter, with none of the other stuff." She reveals

Luca smiles. "Nope. You are one hundred percent, the Don's daughter, recognized by the Council and everything." Milan's smile gets bigger.

"So, who would I have to marry? Have you met him?"

She asks.

"I have. The marriage would be to Ivan."

"The future Pakhan?" She questions.

Luca nods. "Yes. He is a few years older than me I believe. He appears to value family, and declared he would honor his marriage vows."

"Wow." Her jaw is dropped in surprise.

"I want you to know, that I have not agreed on your behalf." Adds Luca.

"But you will?"

"Not without your consent. Or Val's. Ivan gave us two option, a wife for him, or a husband for his Second's little sister. She is only eight so Val would have some time before he's married. Yours would take place shortly after you turn eighteen." Replies Luca. "I don't need an answer today. I want you both to think on it. And let me know if you have any questions."

With that, Luca leaves the room. Neither Milan nor I move.

"Wow." She says.

I can only nod. Shit. Fuck. What do I do if Milan says no, I will have to agree, then if I find Keira, what the fuck would I do.

"You're thinking awfully hard over there. Care to share?" She asks.

I run my fingers threw my hair. "There's someone from my past I'm trying to find. I think Santo might have had something to do with it."

"You loved her." I can't help the recoil my body does at her words. How the hell did she know that? I stare at her for a moment before she laughs and continues. "You looked stressed, angry even at the prospect of an arranged marriage. But I know you. You are loyal to the family. If Luca asked

44

you to do it, you would do it. So that had to mean you didn't want the marriage, because you had someone else in mind."

"When the hell did you get so smart?" I tease.

Her smile turns sad. "The day I got to start thinking and acting for myself."

"And that's another reason I would do it Milan. You have had enough choices taken away from you. I don't want this to be another one."

She stands and moves to sit beside me. Taking one of my hands in hers. It's comforting. Almost motherly. "Val. I grew up as the Don's daughter. I've had an arranged marriage in place since I was eight. I knew I would never choose my husband. I accepted that long ago. Did I for a time hope it would be to Luca? Yes. Because Luca would have been polite to me, even if he ignored me. He wouldn't have thrown mistresses in my face, or breed an army of children he never intended to get to know. Would I have loved Luca, probably not. But I would have admired and respected him. By the sounds of it, I could have that with Ivan. We don't know him, so I can't be sure. But the chance is there for me."

"I can dig into him for you. Find any skeletons in his closet." I offer.

She smiles appreciatively. "Thank you Val. I would like that. In the meantime, I hope you find the one you are looking for." Giving my hand one last squeeze, she stands and heads for the door.

"Are you sure about this Milan?" I call to her. "We don't have to give an answer yet."

"Then we won't, but if Luca asks before you decide, I will accept Ivan's offer."

CHAPTER SEVEN

Val

It's been a week since the incident at the marina. We're just leaving the Russian's restaurant. Luca, Massimo and I are all in separate cars with our own escorts. We've been making plans to go after the Cartel. I'm curious as to why Ivan hasn't asked about the arranged marriage deal. Truthfully, it's probably a good thing he didn't. I'm not sure Luca has an answer.

I think Luca's waiting for me to sway the vote one way or another. I don't have an answer for him. I need my mind at peace with what went down seven years ago first.

I'm getting close to finding the truth about Keira. I can feel it. I finally had time this past week to dig further into the doctor I found. She doesn't have any social media so photos have been nearly impossible to get. I've found a few but they're either side profiles or blurry. It's hard to tell if it's my Keira. It's been seven years. We both would have changed a lot. Our features matured. Hell I'm twice the size I was back then. A few inches in height and the rest in muscle. I'm nowhere near the size of Luca or Massimo, but considering how scrawny of a teen I was, I look huge in comparison.

Coincidentally, the woman started working in the hospital the Caruso Family owns about six months ago. I hacked into the system and found out her schedule. She's working tonight. I plan on going to visit her. I need to know is it's really her, or if I'm hunting a ghost that died seven years ago.

I go to church like a good Italian boy, but I've never done much praying. I am today. I'm praying that this doctor is my Keira. I've combed the Internet and the dark web. This is my only lead. If she's not her. If my girl is really dead, I don't know what I'll do. Hell, even if she's alive and this is her, I still don't know what I'll do.

Bam. Something hits my door with enough force to rock the car. "What the fuck was that?" I ask to no one in particular.

Before any of the guards accompanying me can respond, we are hit again. And again. Shit. Gunfire. We are under attack. I pull out my phone to call for back-up. It flies out of my hands before I can hit send as something explodes beneath our car. My head smacks against the roof that is collapsing in on me each time we flip.

Finally we come to a stop. Pain radiates through my ribs as I struggle to unlatch my seatbelt. I'm thankful I wore it. I can see Sammy, one of my guards wasn't so lucky. He wasn't wearing his belt, and he's no longer seated beside me, or in the car at all. As the belt breaks free, I slam down onto the remains of the roof. More gunfire rings out and pings against the door. They are reinforced. The windows were bullet proof but several seem to have been taken out while we were rolling.

I take a quick stock of my injuries, weapons and

surroundings. My ribs hurt but don't seem broken, my phone is missing, I have my gun and another clip in my jacket. Emilio, my driver is dead. Sounds like Nick, another one of my guards is outside the car returning fire. The car's distress beacon should be relaying our location so back-up should be arriving soon. I just need to hold on long enough for Luca or Massimo to get to me.

Unless they are under attack too.

Fuck!

Time to fight.

I crawl out of the car on the side not taking hits. Nick is there, crouched behind the tire that's still slightly spinning, firing at our attackers. He gives me a nod as I move to his side. "How many?" I ask.

"Eight." He replies. "Maybe more."

"Shit. What about our escorts?" We were traveling with two other cars. It's our standard procedure.

The grim look in his eyes already lets me know its bad news. "They've got car one pinned down. They were run off the road. Car burst into flames. Not sure if anyone made it out. We rolled a hell of a ways away from three. They're about two hundred yards to our west taking fire, but it looks like we're their primary target. Or should I say you."

There's a break in their shooting. I turn at the same time as Nick to fire off a few rounds. Looking through the smoke that's beginning to fill the street, I can see a few men on the move, inching closer to us. With each pull of the trigger, I feel my inner beast that thirsts for blood getting closer to the surface. I'd normally be working to calm myself down, bury the beast back into the far recesses of my mind. Not today. Today I need to set him free. These assholes have been fucking with our city for too long. It ends now.

Unleashing the beast, I take out two with my gun, before

moving out from behind our car. Nick tries to stop me but I shrug him off. These men don't seem to be aiming to kill me. My soldiers, yes. Me, no. They plan to take me alive.

Not happening. The red haze of rage in my vision isn't hindering me like it should, it's amplifying every one of my senses.

I make my way to the sidewalk and creep along behind the cars while Nick continues to lay down cover fire. I get myself behind two of the bastards. My gun is out of bullets, but I don't care. It won't stop me.

I pull my knife from the sheathe at my ankle, then slice through the first man's neck with ease. I keep hold of the body to use as a shield. The second turns and tries to shoot me. His ex-buddy takes the brunt of the bullets. One must go through his carcass, as there is a burning pain in my side.

No time for pain.

I drop the body and lunge at the second while he tries to replace his empty clip. I'm faster. And I'm pissed. I stab him repeatedly in the abdomen. I'm so focused on my task that I forget that there are still more enemies lingering nearby. They get the jump on me.

Two try to grab me but I fight back. A third tackles us all to the ground. I'm almost loose when someone Tasers me. The electricity sends my body to the ground in an angry fit. Zip ties are snapped into place around my ankles and my wrist. I can't give up. I can't let them take me. The more I struggle, the harder I'm kicked and punched. Everything hurts.

Fuck. I don't have time for this. I'm supposed to find my girl today. I need to find my girl. I need to know what Santo did to her.

Because with every passing day I am more and more convinced that he did do something. I just hope it's something we can come back from, and that she hasn't moved on.

I haven't.

CHAPTER EIGHT

Keira

I should not have sparred with Grady before my shift today. What should have been a twelve hour shift turned into sixteen. I am dead on my feet and all I want is some greasy food and a long soak in my tub. Pulling out my phone, I shoot Killian a text to let him know I'm on my way home, and see if he'll order a pizza for me. His response comes back in seconds. "I got you babe."

As my car comes into view in the parking lot, I stuff my phone in my bag and dig for my keys. Just as I get them out, a dark SUV screeches to a stop next to me. Two men in suits jump out. I wait for them to attack me. They'll be sorry when they do.

"Dr. Jones?" The one asks as he takes one step closer to me. I don't answer. He takes another step closer and grabs my badge that was clasped to my scrubs. Acting on instinct, I swing my fist. It connects with his cheek and splits his lip. Instead of attacking in return as I expected, he takes a step back and grabs a handkerchief from his pocket. He dabs at the few drops of blood, then returns his focus to my badge. The damn thing gives me away. "You've got a mean swing Doc. I wish I had the time to explain, but I need you to come with me."

I start to back away. I don't get far. There must have been a third guy in the car that circled around behind me, because I back up right into a hard body. Before my mind has time to process the danger, a pair of zip-ties are tightened around my wrist and a bag is thrown over my head.

The brute then throws me over his shoulder. I kick and scream. I fight with everything I have, but once I'm in the vehicle, they restrain my legs. I continue to scream until I'm hoarse. With the bag over my head I can't tell where we are going. They haven't really hurt me yet, but they could be waiting until they get me wherever we are going. Deciding to focus my attention on learning more about my captors and our destination, I stop screaming. "What do you want with me? Why are you doing this?"

"You'll find out when we get there." Says someone to my right. It wasn't the one who spoke to me earlier.

"Why can't you tell me now?"

"It's need to know. Boss told us to find you and bring you back to the compound."

"I haven't done anything."

The man grunts. "Didn't say you did."

I wish the bag wasn't on my head so I could give him an incredulous look. "Then why was I kidnapped?"

"Time was of the essence. I had started to ask nicely. You became defensive quickly. I admire your tenacity, but I didn't have time for it. I apologize for the theatrics. Once we get inside, I can release you." I feel the car slowing down. "Do me a favor. Don't provoke the boss. He's not in the best of moods. He'll make what I've done seem like an afternoon tea with Granny."

"My Granny was a bitch, and liked bourbon not tea."

The man snorts as the car comes to a stop. I'm lifted from the vehicle and thrown back over a shoulder. I don't fight this time. I'm tired and sore, and I have a feeling I'm going to need whatever strength I have left for what is to come.

I can feel the air pressure around me change. We've entered a building. The man continues walking for about thirty paces before turning and descending some stairs.

There is a hell of a commotion going on somewhere ahead of us. The bag is still on my head so I can't see, but I get the distinct smell of blood and disinfectant wafting into my nose. Strangely it smells much like an operating room.

"Got some help for you Doc." Hollers the man holding me as he drops me to my feet. Thankfully he had the good sense to keep hold of me or I would have crashed to the floor.

"Jesus, did you kidnap her?" The voice sounds familiar but I can't pinpoint who it is.

"You said it was urgent. She was asking questions and trying to get in her car to leave. What else should I have done?"

The other man huffs before saying, "take the damn bag off her head."

The man follows the order. Unfortunately he leaves my hands and legs tied. Blinking a few times from the brightness of the lights, my eyes start to focus and land on the man who gave the order to remove the bag. He's a doctor at the hospital. "Dr. Moro what the hell is going on?"

"Sorry Dr. Jones, I don't have time to explain everything. I need your help, and he asked for you specifically."

Looking around the room I don't see anyone I recognize. Turning my attention back to Dr. Moro, I see his hands are covered in blood. A man is on the table in front of him. Not sure how I missed it before. There is a lot of blood. Too much. I try to step forward to assist, forgetting my legs are still secured together. "Hey Goliath," I say to the man still holding me up. He looks down at me with a scowl. "You going to untie me so I can help?"

The man says nothing, but turns to another man in a suit who steps out of the shadows. He's got a gun strapped to his hip. I don't know his name, but I know the type of man he is. Mafia. Fuck. How did I get involved in this? If this has anything to do with Killian I'm going to kick his ass. Are these guys Irish, Russian, or Italian? It's hard to say. From what I know, they all tend to wear suits, scowls, guns, and tattoos.

The man in the corned says nothing. His eyes rove over me. Sizing me up. He must decide I'm not a threat, or that he can always kill me later if I am, because he gives Goliath a nod who then proceeds to cut off the zip ties on my hands and feet.

I rub at my wrist to calm the sting as I walk over to the sink. Working quickly I get my hands sterilized and slide on some gloves. The man on the table looks like he took one hell of a beating. His face is so swollen and bruised, I'm not sure even his own mother would recognize him right now.

While his face looks like shit, it's his chest and abdomen that are the main concern. Dr. Moro's has a pair of forceps deep in what appears to be a bullet wound. Lower down the man has multiple gashes that look like someone tried to carve him like a Thanksgiving turkey. Good news is, the bulk of the blood I see is dried, and may not all be his.

Dr. Moro looks like he is struggling. I gently take the tools out of his hands, then roughly bump him out of the way with my hip. The boss man in the corner doesn't like this and immediately draws his gun on me. I don't flinch. It's not the first time someone's drawn one on me. I doubt it will be the last, unless he decides to shoot. I ignore him for the moment and grab the spotlight and drag it closer. I can see the glint of the bullet lodged in the man's chest. "Either put one in my head and two in the chest, or put the damn toy away. If I wanted to kill him, I could have done it four different ways already." I say gruffly as I notice the man still has it aimed at me.

I shouldn't provoke the man with a gun. Logically I know this, but he's pissing me off, and I'm tired and hungry, it's a bad combination.

My forceps latch onto the bullet. I pull it out slowly. Not wanting to hit or nick anything as I pull it out. Dr. Moro is at my side with a dish. I plop it in as Doc gives the bullet a rinse. "Fuck." We both say together.

"What, what is it?" Asks Boss Man as he joins me across the table, but I pay him no mind as I get back to work.

"Luca," Doc says to the man. "The bullet is fractured. There is a piece still inside your brother."

"Doc, do you have any blood for a transfusion?" I ask. He can explain the specifics of what I need to do later. This is urgent. If this goes sideways, he's going to need blood. No, he's going to need it either way.

He shakes his head. "No. We usually take the men to the hospital. It wasn't safe for Val to go there. We usually only have minor injuries we deal with at the compound." I've got the forceps back in Val's chest. I think I see a glimmer of metal. Please be the bullet.

Wait.

Val? Luca?

Shit. Fuck.

"You can't let him die." Says Luca.

Holy shit. "Is your brother's name Valentino?" I don't

look up. My eyes are frozen on the face of the man who's bruised and beaten.

"Yes." He says. His voice stretching the word. I can detect anger as well as confusion at my question.

"Valentino Mariani?"

"How the fuck do you know that name?" It's strange. He both whispers and yells the question. Or maybe it's the blood pumping loudly in my ears that makes me think he whispered.

The forceps clamp down on the bullet fragment. It didn't puncture anything. I pull it out gently and toss it and my tools down. "Start closing him up." I bark to Dr. Moro. It takes him a moment to snap out of his stupor. Turning to Goliath, I ask. "What's your blood type?"

He looks at Luca, then at me. "A positive."

Turning to the next monkey in the suit I ask the same thing. He's not a match either. Shit. The other two in the room don't know theirs. Turning to Luca, he answers before I can ask him. "I'm AB negative, and he's my brother, that means we're a match right?"

"No, you're not." I say with a shake of my head. "Val is B negative."

"How the fuck do you know that?" He growls as he prowls around the table. I ignore him. "Dr. Moro, how far away is the hospital?" He's nearly done stitching Val up. He doesn't look good. Too pale. He has lost too much blood.

Without looking up he answers. "Fifteen minutes."

"I can make it in eight." Says Goliath as he turns and runs from the room. Presumably to go to the hospital. Even at eight minutes there and someone standing at the door with the blood, there will still be the turnaround time of another eight. I fear it will be too late by then.

"Who the fuck are you?" Barks Luca. He's got me pinned

against the counter along the wall. His hand at my neck, and his gun at my temple. I should be scared. I am. Just not of him. I'm scared for Val. For my Tino. I haven't seen him in seven years. He's changed so much. Even with the bruises and blood, I can't believe I didn't recognize him. Now I see him. I only see him.

It's not safe for me to be here, but it's too late for that. I can't let Tino die. I walked away to save him once. Walking away now will kill him. I'd rather be the one to die.

Summoning all the courage I have, which isn't much. I look straight into Luca's eyes. The eyes of the brother of the only man I've ever loved. They are similar to Tino's. I never did get to meet Luca while we were dating. I had wanted to focus on school before we became serious and did the family introductions. Then graduation weekend happened and I had to leave. "I'm Keira."

Luca takes a step back. "Keira. The Keira." His eyes wide with surprise.

I don't answer with words. I only nod. Then turn to gather the supplies I need and jump onto the counter. It's wide enough that I'll be able to lay down on it, and close enough that the tube will reach Luca.

"You." I yell to the man nearest the stairs. "I'm going to need a big glass of juice, some cookies, crackers, or some kind of snack with sugar."

Luca gives him a nod. He's taken a few more steps back from me, his gun now hanging limply in his hand. "On it." Replies the man by the stairs before racing up them and past a man coming down.

I use my teeth to assist with wrapping an elastic band around my upper arm. I find my vein quickly. I've done it more times than I care to think about.

"What the hell is she doing?" Ask the new guy. He's

huge. Bigger than Luca, and he looks like he's two seconds from losing his shit. Or maybe he already lost it, and this is him calming down.

Before Luca can reply, I answer. "I'm a universal donor." I lay back against the counter and remove the elastic.

"What does that...."

I don't wait for him to finish. "It means Tino can take mine. You don't have any blood bags here, no one else is a match, and it will take too long for Goliath to return from the hospital."

The other man returns with the juice and a granola bar. I sit back up long enough to take two huge bites of the bar and chug back about half of the drink. Putting them down and grabbing the other end of the tube with another needle. I stretch them out to Dr. Moro. He takes them without a word, but I can see the questions swirling in his eyes.

"I'm trusting you Doc." He gives me a nod. "I'm going to pass out. Wait until the last second to pull the line. Pull too early and he'll die. Bleed me dry and I'll come back and haunt your ass. Got me." I wiggle to get myself as comfortable as possible while Dr. Moro connects the line to Tino.

"Thank you Dr. Jones." Whisper Dr. Moro.

I give him a nod, then turn to look at Luca. I can feel the shadows creeping into my vision already. "It's Keira, Doctor. Keira Harlow." I whisper before the darkness takes over.

CHAPTER NINE

Val

Holy fuck that hurts. Everything hurts.

Holy shit. I'm alive. How? Why?

I try to think back to the last thing I remember. A gunfight. Our car flipping over. Joseph. And Ramirez. He was there. In the house. My brain is foggy. It hurts to concentrate. I'm not still there am I?

I try to open my eyes. It's bright and my eyes rebel. They want to remain closed. I give up and let them. I turn my attention to feeling around me. I'm on something soft. A bed. I have a sheet on me. A pillow is under my head. It's soft. Really soft.

They wouldn't have me in a bed. Would they?

No, Ramirez wanted me to suffer. Memories flood forward. Being tied to a chair. Cut with a knife. He wanted to know who sold him out. Who we had on the inside. Then he stopped and took a phone call. He was bitching to someone about Joseph having grabbed a girl. Then he shot me.

I was shot. My hand tries to move to search for the

wound, but a pull on my forearm stops me. Looking down I see an IV in my arm. Why? Or was I saved? Did Luca find me?

There are voices coming from outside the door. I close my eyes again and try to relax. Until I know who I am dealing with, I don't want them to realize I've woken up. For all I know, I'm still in that godforsaken place, and they are fixing me up, so they can beat me again. It's a tactic our family has done in the past. If I can fake being asleep long enough, maybe I can get enough energy to escape.

The door to the room is opened loudly. A female voice hushes the others. I don't recognize it. Or I don't think I do. My head hurts too much. It's taking everything in me not to let out a groan of pain.

"Why isn't he waking up?" I know that voice. Hang on. I know the name.

Stupid brain. Work.

"I told you he might not wake up for hours. Everyone comes out of it different. It's not an exact science." Whose voice was that? It's the female again. Something about it is familiar. The names are there, in my mind, but it's like they float away before I can grab onto them. "He had two fractured ribs, six knife wounds, a broken wrist, a nicked artery, a severe concussion, and multiple contusions and lacerations all over his body. Honestly it's a miracle he's alive."

"And he better fucking stay that way."

"Why would I save his life just to kill him now?" Argues the female. "If I wanted him dead I would have let him bleed out, or before that I could have let the bullet slip and fuck up his artery more, or I could have pumped him with the wrong medication, smothered him with a pillow, or grabbed someone's gun and shot him."

"Alright I get it." Luca says with a heavy sigh. That's it! Luca. My brother Luca. I'm safe. Holy shit. I'm safe. I open my eyes slowly, knowing the bright light is going to hurt my eyes and head even more.

"Thank you Doctor. Truly, you've gone above and beyond for my son." That's the voice of my dad.

"You're welcome." Her voice sounds tired. "Now, can I please leave?"

"No." Reply Luca and dad together.

Huh, I wonder what their deal is with the Doctor. Is it me? Am I the reason she can't leave? What the hell else is wrong with me? They said I've been here two weeks, I should be on the mend, right?

"Why the hell not?" She screeches. You can hear the anger as well as a tinge of fear in her voice.

Why indeed? "Elena's still running your background check." Luca answers.

Where is our usual Doctor? Dr. Moro.

"Why the hell do you need a background check? You know where I work. Where my apartment is. And I just pointed out all the ways I could have killed him and didn't. What more could you want?"

"I want to know where you've been the last seven years. We have a lot of enemies. We need to be sure you aren't one of them." Seven years. That's oddly specific.

Seven. Why does that number ring a bell?

"Enemies? You think I'd hurt him?" The confusion and sadness is clear in her voice.

"Haven't you?"

Their fighting isn't helping my head. I need them to shut up, or leave the room. Or both. And I need to get back to work.

What the fuck was I working on? "Ugh." I can't help the

groan that escapes my mouth this time.

"Val? Thank fuck." Luca says as he rushes over to where I'm lying.

"Most people would thank god." Not sure where that snappy comeback came from, but I like it. I laugh. It's delayed. Fuck them. I have a head injury.

"He's still not funny." That's a new female voice. I know this one. Milan. I turn to the door. Sure enough, there she is. I wave her over. There are tears in her eyes. She wipes them away before they fall.

"Hey…" I say calmly. "What happened?" I reach out for her hand. She takes it. We never used to be close. Her mother was a vicious conniving woman who controlled everything Milan did. From the clothes, to the make-up and heels. Yes, the girl was forced to wear make-up and heels starting at the age of twelve. Her mother was grooming her. Thank fuck her mother isn't around anymore.

Huh, I guess "thank fuck" is a saying people say.

With tears still lingering in her eyes, she answers me. "You were kidnapped."

I give a little laugh but then groan when it hurts too much. "Yeah, I remember that part." I try to shift to get a bit more comfortable. The first female, the Doctor, is at my side helping me. There is something familiar about her. I still can't remember why. "I meant how did I get back here? How did you all find me?"

"Livianna volunteered to be kidnapped." Milan replies.

My eyes involuntarily bug out. "What?" Luca curses. Elena laughs from the doorway as she and Livianna enter the room. Massimo is a few steps behind her.

Livianna steps up to my side and plants a gentle kiss on my cheek. Shit even that hurts.

"I wasn't planning on getting kidnapped." She huffs. "It

was supposed to be one final field mission. Find Joseph, get him to talk. I knew there were risks. We were prepared. We had back-up this time." She explains as Massimo steps up to her back. His arms wrap around her and pulls her close. I see Luca doing the same with Elena at the end of my bed. The Doctor has stepped back. She's shrouded in shadows now. "They brought me to the same place as you. I was only there a few minutes before the house was surrounded."

"Are you okay?" My eyes scan over her. She has a few old looking bruises on her arms and a small cut on her forehead that looks mostly healed. "Did they hurt you?" It feels like a stupid question even as I ask it. Of course they hurt her.

"Few bumps and bruises. Nothing major." I'm not sure if she's telling me the truth. Looking to Massimo, he doesn't look ready to commit mass murder, so it must be true.

"Good." I say with a nod. Nope. Don't nod. I'm instantly nauseous. I close my eyes in the hopes it helps it pass. "Don't you dare do that again."

"If it means saving..." She begins a rebuttal. I don't want to hear it. I don't ever want her or any other female in our family hurt.

I don't wait for her to finish. "No." I say sternly. I open my eyes. Making sure to make direct eye contact with her. "Never. You leave me." I then look to Elena, and finally Milan. "Understood?" They don't respond. "You find another way to save me, or you leave me. Got it?"

"No." Says Elena while Milan and Livianna nod along. "We're a family Val. We don't leave family like that." The conviction in her voice is hard to argue against. So I don't. I'm also too tired, and I have a feeling none of them will be leaving the compound without an army to escort them for a very long time.

My energy is fading fast. The bed is comfy, but I'm not. I need something. I try to move to fix it. I only succeed in groaning again. The Doctor moves out of the shadows and to my bedside. "That's enough." She says as she helps me to lift my upper body and stuff another pillow behind me. Then she takes a second and third pillow and stuffs one under each of my arms to prop them up. Huh. That feels pretty good. "He needs to rest. He still has a long way to heal."

No one argues. They all look tired too.

Luca squeezes my shoulder before leading Elena and Milan out of the room. The girls both give me a wave over their shoulders. Massimo leans in to bump my knuckles gently. Livianna repeats the move but with a smile before they leave.

Dad steps up last. He gives my shoulder a squeeze. The familiarity of the move washes away any pain it gives me. I really am home. Safe. For now. "Glad to see you awake son."

Before he shuts the door behind him, leaving the Doctor in the room with me, she whispers to him. "Can I go home now? Please, people will be looking for me."

"Let them. They won't find you until we want them to." With that said, Dad leaves the room.

The Doc flops into the chair in the corner. I try to get a better look at her. There is something familiar about her, but I still can't figure it out. She's beautiful. Even with dark circles under her eyes. She's got her long brown hair pulled into a messy bun atop her head. A few pieces have fallen out and circle her heart shaped face. Her eyes look green, maybe hazel. I once knew a girl with beautiful emerald eyes.

My eyelids grow too heavy to keep open, so I close them and let the memories take me away. Everything else is still hard to concentrate on. Not her though. Never her. I can see my girl clearly in my mind as I drift to sleep.

CHAPTER TEN

Keira

It's been two days since Val woke up. I'm still not allowed to go home, let alone leave the basement. Though, that's probably due to my failed escape attempts.

At the beginning of my stay here, I had been given a room on the second floor. There was a guard outside the door to the room, not wanting to hurt him, I opted to go out the window. I didn't have any rope so I tied the bed sheets together and hooked them to the leg of the bed. It wasn't long enough for me to reach the ground, but it got me close enough to be able to jump without hurting myself. Once on the ground I took off running. I got about halfway to the large stone wall before I was surrounded by ATVs. Luca joined them in a golf cart a minute later. He escorted me back to the house. This time I was given a room on the ground floor. The windows were barred and too narrow to escape through.

I contained my eagerness to escape for three days. My plan was to convince them that I wasn't going to attempt to run again. On the third night, when I thought it late enough for everyone to be in bed, I picked the lock on the door. Opening it as quietly as I could, I surprised the guard by jumping on his back and quickly locking my arms around his neck in a choke-hold. He took a minute to lose consciousness. The moment he did, I took off running again. This time, I only made it as far as the back deck before the flood lights became spotlights.

Three men came rushing out of the house, I put up a fight. I had gotten several good kicks and punches in before I was forced to the ground. Once the handcuffs locked into place. I knew my fight was over again. Little did I know, I wouldn't get the chance to try again.

This time I didn't get placed in a bedroom. I was given a closet with a mat on the floor with a single pillow and scratchy blanket. There was no window and no door handle on the inside of the closet. To use the bathroom or be let out of the closet, I had to knock on the door. It was humiliating.

I tried to use it to fuel the fire within me, but all that did was piss me off more since I didn't have a proper outlet for my emotions anymore. It has been weeks since I fought or sparred anyone. Hell, I would settle for a punching bag or a treadmill if it meant I could burn off some of the excess energy I had.

I've still been tending to Val. Though I try to time it to coincide with his frequent naps. He has made a few attempts to talk to me when he rouses, but I quickly make an excuse to leave. I also don't make eye contact and have been leaving my hair down to create a curtain between us when I need to be close. He hasn't mentioned our past, or made any indication that he recognizes me.

Luca knows my true identity. He knows who I once was to Val. Surprisingly he hasn't mentioned anything to him. I'm not sure what he's waiting for. If he's waiting for me to say something, he will be waiting forever. I need to leave. Being with Val isn't safe for him. I was warned years ago. I won't let him be hurt. Not if I can help it. I still love him. Even though it's been years since we saw each other last. Even though he's probably moved on a hundred times over the years. Even if he never knew I loved him. I never told him. I was afraid. My parents were the last ones I told I love you to.

I should have told Val. I should have grabbed onto every opportunity to be with him when I had the chance.

It's too late for us.

I've been staring at the wall for an hour. I'm beginning to lose my mind. It's too quiet here. I have too much time to think. Time to fret. My nerves are shot. I need a fight, or someone to spar with. Hell, I've done two hundred push-ups and sit-ups this morning already just to burn off some of my feelings.

I had hoped Killian would have found me by now. Or maybe he has, but can't get to me. He wouldn't attack the Caruso compound to get me. He's not suicidal. I'd call him if I were allowed. They took my phone, my bag. I have no way to contact anyone in the outside world.

The only escape attempt I've been able to conjure that has a fraction of a possibility of working is to set a fire down here. The alarms would go off and they would scramble to get Val to safety. While preoccupied with him and putting the fire out, I could make my escape.

The plan has a dozen ways it could fail. Maybe even more like a hundred ways. And with even one of those alleged failures resulting in Val getting hurt, I won't risk it. So here I'll sit. Here I'll stay. Slowly going insane.

A knock at the door tells me it must be lunch time. I don't bother to tell them to come in. They'll do it anyway.

Like predicted, the door opens. It's Livianna only she's not carrying a tray this time. I've come to realize that she had an uncanny ability to read when someone is lying. She's also super sweet and theirs an aura about her that relaxes you. Makes you want to tell her your deepest darkest secrets. It's obnoxious.

I know that's why they've been sending her to feed me. They want me to talk. I won't. I've spent years being quiet. "Hey Doc. You want to take a walk? Get out of this room."

I don't verbalize an answer. I act as nonchalant as I can as I get up from the make-shift bed, and follow her out the door. She doesn't lead me to the stairs, but rather the other way. Deeper into the belly of the basement. I've done it before. When I first got here and had more freedom, I explored all the rooms without locked doors.

She leads me to the kitchenette at the end of the hall. The doors along the hallway are usually shut and locked. I've checked. Multiple times. A few times I've gotten glimpses of the rooms. One is an armory. Another is the indoor gun range. There is a room with a dozen monitors or so. I'm guessing security.

Just before the kitchenette, a new door is open today. I can hear grunts and the familiar sounds of weights clanging. It's a gym. Fuck yes.

I immediately stop. Liv notices. "You want to go in?" She asks. "There's treadmills along the back wall if you want to use one."

The treadmill isn't what I have my eye on. It's the boxing ring that's dead center in the room. I don't bother replying to Liv before making my way to the ring. A massive man stands in the middle of the ring. His back is to us. He's about the same size as the last guy I fought in the underground.

Another guy enters the ring. They tap gloves then circle

each other for a moment. I recognize the big guy. It's Massimo, Livianna's boyfriend. I watch as the two men throw a series of well-choreographed punches and kicks. Massimo is quick for his size. Not highly flexible though. Taking out his legs a couple times and having his body weight crash to the ground a few times will slow him down. Then a takedown should be easy.

I tear my eyes from the men. I've seen enough for the moment. Moving to the bench, I find the tape and go to work wrapping my hands. Livianna comes up beside me. Asking me what I'm doing. And am I seriously considering getting in the ring with one of the guys.

"Yep." I reply.

The guys around the room have crowed around the ring. They begin to cheer.

With my hands ready to go, I return my focus to the match. Just as I thought. Massimo wins.

Good.

I whip off my t-shirt. Thank goodness they gave me some leggings and sports bras to wear. They might see my scars, but who cares. The shirt is too confining to fight in, and I need this adrenaline rush.

The fallen man is helped from the ring. Massimo stands in the middle. "Who's next?" He asks. His cockiness draws me to the ropes. I love when the big men fall. I would have been happy fighting anyone. But his preening is making the rush I feel double.

My turn to play.

Without a word, I jump into the ring before anyone else can. Bouncing on my toes, as is my ritual to get my blood pumping. I ready myself. Any punch he lands is going to hurt. With me being a girl, he might pull his punches at first.

I bet I can get him to stop after I land a few of my own

hits. I won't hold back.

"You best get out of this ring little girl before you get hurt." He says with a hint of laughter in his voice.

Not letting it affect me. I'm used to men underestimating me. I take two steps forward, tap his gloves with my knuckles as I reply "not a little girl." Then I land my left hook to his right cheek.

He stumbles back a step, clearly not expecting me to hit him, let alone as hard as I did. I'm not the champion of the underground for no reason. He recovers from his shock quickly. I've poked the beast. Good. "Oh, you want to play?" He says as he finally gets into fighting position.

"No. I want to fight." I retort as I lunge at him, knowing he will take the bait. I'm quicker though. In a flash, I change course and end up behind him. I drop to the floor and sweep out his legs. He crashes down. Hard.

"Yes!" I hear Livianna yell. Then the familiar rumblings of men placing bets.

"Liv!" Barks Massimo as he shoots a look of betrayal at her. There was venom in his eyes when he was looking at me, but they soften when they lock eyes. I had that once. Or thought I did.

Killian gives me looks, not of love, but rather lust and kinship. I know he cares for me. As I do him. We are bonded by tragedy and pain. No one understands me like him.

Massimo gets up. We circle each other for a few minutes both throwing punches and kicks. Not really doing any damage. I'm sure he's still holding back. I can get him to stop.

I let him think he's backing me into the corner. Then I dive underneath him, roll onto my back and kick at the back of his knees. That sends him to the mat again. He's quick to recover. I'm already back on my feet waiting for him. He throws several combinations before he lands a solid punch to my jaw. I feel my lip split. A smile breaches my face. The pain wakes me up. It's what I've been missing the last few weeks.

The gym is dead silent. Massimo looks stunned that he hit me. Can't have that.

While he's still frozen, I roundhouse kick him. He staggers back. Before he can recover, I've got him on his back on the mat. My arms locking him in a chock-hold. This is where his flexibility hinders him the most. He can't get his arms to get a good enough grip on me, and with the way his legs are positioned, he's struggling to get his footing under him.

Before he can pass out. He manages to roll us. It's the only move he had to make, and I was anticipating it.

He gets on all four, with me on his back, just as the doors slam open. "What the fuck is going on here!" Fucking Luca. He's ruining my fun.

Daring to glance over to him, without releasing my hold, I connect eyes with Val, he's standing beside Luca. His eyes burning with anger. Why the hell is he mad?

I return my focus to Massimo. With my arms around his neck, I manage to pull back a knee and jam it forward into his kidney. He roars in pain.

That managed to piss him off. I feel his muscles clench before I realize what his plan is. I don't have time to prepare. With all of his might, he throws himself backwards. Crushing me to the mat with his entire weight on top of me.

Any air I had in my lungs goes rushing out.

Fuck. That hurt.

I still have hold of his neck, but my grip is weak. Massimo disengages my arms with a gentleness I didn't know he possessed. After getting back on his feet, he gives me a smile and offers me a hand. Knowing our fight is over for now, and that I have finally been defeated, I take it and let him help me up.

"Not bad little girl." I smile at him and tap his gloves again. Before turning to the murderous gaze of Luca, Ricco, and Bosco. I hadn't realized the last two had entered the room as well.

Val is behind them. He doesn't look angry. He looks stunned. Before I can further evaluate the meaning of his look, Liv jumps into the ring and throws her arms around me. "That was amazing! I've never seen Mass take so many hits from anyone. Let alone a woman."

"Uh...thanks." I'm not sure what the proper response should be for praising me for hitting her man. Shouldn't she be mad?

"Can you teach me?" She asks.

Before I can answer, Massimo jumps in. "Absolutely not."

"Why? She's really good. Do you have any idea how much I could learn?" Livianna rebuts.

"Yes I do. But you're pregnant. You are not getting in the ring until after the baby is born. Maybe not even then."

"I can wait to get in the ring until the baby is born." She says softly while rubbing her flat stomach. "I could just learn and practice for now. I only know some self-defense. Elena knows how to fight, why can't I?"

Massimo pulls her away from my side. He pulls her close and brushes a few strands of hair behind her ear. "Because you don't need to."

"Why, because I won't be kidnapped? Been there." She grumbles. "Done that."

"Liv...." He begins to scold, though there isn't any real heat in his voice.

"No Mass. I get that you want to protect me."

"I will protect you." He replies adamantly.

"I know. But I'd like to have the security of knowing I can put up a good fight." He's caving. You can see the tight muscles in his jaw relaxing.

"I can teach you some things." I pipe in. Then, before Massimo can remind me she's pregnant, I continue, "No impact. Just technique, combinations. We could watch some of the guys and I can give her pointers on seeing weaknesses."

"Yes!" She shouts while Massimo says "maybe."

Livianna grabs his faces and plants a kiss on his lips. It gets heated quickly. Ripping his lips from hers, Massimo grabs her waist and helps her over the ropes and onto the floor.

I follow suit, ripping the tape off my hands as I head over to my discarded shirt. I can feel the stares on me. The men are no doubt whispering about my scars and making assumptions about how I got them. They probably think what I allow everyone to believe. That I got them fighting. I turn my back so I don't have to deal with it yet. It's childish, but whatever. I don't owe them an explanation. I'm still their prisoner.

"Keira." His voice is barely above a whisper and I freeze. Then a hand is on my shoulder. Turning me to face him. "Keira. My Keira."

CHAPTER ELEVEN
Val

How the hell did I not recognize her? She was once the only one I saw. In a room full of people I could pinpoint her in seconds. It's like my body was attuned to hers. In a way it still is. I had felt an instant attraction to her when the fog had cleared from my head and I could think straight again. Since she refused to be in the room with me longer than she had to, and wouldn't look me in the eye, I had chalked my attraction up to her being a beautiful woman who was nursing me back to health.

Seeing her now. In the ring, throwing kicks and dodging jabs with Massimo, my heart stopped. My girl was not a violent person. What the fuck happened? What has she been through the last few years?

I stalk closer to her. That's when I see it. The scars. The numerous raised bumps along her back. A few look deeper than the others and have a pink tint to them. Fury builds in my gut. Someone hurt my girl.

Fuck. I allowed her to be in a position for her to be hurt. I was supposed to protect her. I should have gone after her. I failed her. Never again.

Never. Fucking. Again. She's never leaving me again. I don't care if she has a man, husband, or fuck buddy. As of this moment, they are done. She's mine, and I don't share. I lost seven years with her. I won't lose another minute.

Their fight is over. Livianna's talking to her. I can't hear a word that is said. My mind is swirling with ideas on how to keep her. Ways to punish those who hurt her.

Santo.

That bastard had something to do with this. I know it. He's lucky he's dead. The ideas for retribution swirling in my head would make even the devil nervous.

Without a doubt, I know it's her. Same emerald eyes, same button nose, and heart-shaped face, though missing the baby fat she once had on her cheeks. It's my mark that confirms it. The tattoo she got that declared her mine. We had it done the week of finals. She has the Caruso insignia along with my name below it "Tino". She hadn't known what it meant then. She trusted me to pick it out for her. Just like I trusted her to pick out mine. A black rose on my chest. Above my heart with her name etched into the stem.

She steps out of the ring. I need to feel her. Touch her. I need my hands on her to be sure she's real. That she's not a ghost.

Slowly I move to her. "Keira." I place a hand on her shoulder and spin her to face me. "My Keira." The words come out in a whisper.

She rips out of my hold, and turns to walk away from me. It's then that I see it. The tattoo isn't the same, or rather it is, but it is disfigured. A large scar runs through it.

"You tried to erase me?" I can't contain the anger in my voice. Not only did she run from me, but she fucking tried to erase my mark.

She stops and turns to face me again. Folding her arms across her chest. "If I had had a choice I would have done a better job?" She replies dryly.

"What?"

"You think I wanted to be sliced and diced? That I asked for this?" Her voice is raised. Not yet a scream. I can feel the anger pouring off of her. She yanks the shirt off her head again, and turns to show me her back again. "You think I wanted to be attacked in my apartment? To have to go on the run, and spend a year on the streets?"

I can't help myself, it's like my hands have a mind of their own as they reach out and touch the scars. Tracing the one through my mark.

She jerks away from my touch. "I need to go. I need to leave." She tries to rush for the door. Bosco and Ricco are there. Blocking her way without me needing to ask. She stops a few feet from them and turns to face Luca who is standing off to the side. "Please let me go."

His only response is to shake his head. He won't let her leave without my approval. And I won't give it.

"What happened that night?"

She doesn't answer. She looks like she's holding back tears. Her head is ducked. Her breathing heavy.

"Keira." I say with force. "Tell me."

"I went to the lake house. Just like we planned. I was in the kitchen, putting away the groceries I had brought with me. I was going to make lasagna for you." I loved her lasagna. "When I turned around, there was a man. I asked him who he was. Stupidly I thought it might be your father. He pulled out a gun. Told me that I needed to leave you. That you were meant for someone else." She must see the confusion on my face because she huffs out a laugh. "Yeah, I didn't believe it either. I knew you weren't always forthcoming with me, but I knew you weren't a liar. There was no way you were with someone else."

Not being able to stand the distance between us anymore, I move closer to her. Giving her time to back away. She doesn't. She stand tall and keeps her eyes locked on mine. I reach out when I get close enough and cup her cheek in my hand. "Never. There was never anyone else. There hasn't been and there never will be."

"What?" I can see the hope shimmering in her eyes. "You've never...but we weren't...and it's been..."

I cut her off with a kiss to her lips. I don't deepen it. I know if I do, I won't be able to stop myself. I've added seven years to my pent up sexual frustration to my raging libido. And it only has eyes for her. "Never. Even when I couldn't have you. I only wanted you."

"I've never either." Her admission shocks the shit out of me and I recoil like I've been tased again. She smiles shyly at me like she can't believe she just admitted it out loud. "There's so much I need to tell you, but you need to know, I've only ever kissed one other person. It didn't mean anything though. He's a friend. He's helped me more than you know."

I lean my forehead against her. I hate that someone else has tasted her lips, but I trust her. If she says it didn't mean anything, than I believe her. And if he truly has helped her, than I won't kill him for tasting what is mine.

"Tell me what happened after that."

"I told him I didn't believe him. He told me I was a stupid girl. So stupid that I didn't realize my boyfriend was in the mafia. Again, I didn't believe him, but he had pictures. A dozen of them. You were covered in blood. I thought at first they were fake. But then he showed me a video. You were torturing a guy. Pounding nails into his hands, then slicing off his fingers. I couldn't watch it all. I ran to the sink to throw up. He came behind. Held the gun to my hand and slapped a pen and piece of paper on the counter next to me and told me to write. To tell you it's over." Her body is shaking. I wrap my arms around her to keep her steady. Trying to pour my strength into her.

It was Santo. He had had his phone out that night during my initiation. I never questioned it. Never thought he was taking photos and videos. My girl was innocent, and she saw my monster. Fuck.

"I didn't want to. You have to believe me. Even after watching what you did to that man, I still wanted you. I knew you would never hurt me, and if you were hurting someone else, it was because they deserved it." Her breathing is choppy, there are tears lingering in her eyes. I can tell my girl doesn't want to cry. That she's trying to be strong.

I lift her into my arms and walk over to the bench. I sit with her straddling me. Chest to chest. I place my hand at the back of her neck and pull her head to my neck. "Let it out. Let go sweetheart. I'm here now. I'm never letting you go."

The damn breaks. Tears pour from her eyes. She struggles to catch her breath as deep sobs wrack her body. I keep a tight hold on her with my arm at her back, and use the other to stroke her hair. Trying to calm her. Over her shoulder I see Ricco and Bosco give a nod then leave the room.

Luca moves to the cabinet along the wall and grabs a towel, then a water from the mini fridge. He brings it over to us. Her crying has seized, her body still shaking. Luca takes the towel and wraps it around her. "Keira." He says gently as he squats down beside us. He puts himself in her field of view, so she doesn't need to turn her head to see him. "Did he hurt you?"

She shakes her head. "Not that night." Instinctively my arms tighten around her. "After I wrote the note, he grabbed my arm and tried to lead me out back. Told me we were going to take a walk. I knew that wasn't really what he meant. He was going to shoot me and hide my body. As we descended the stairs, I took a chance, I threw myself over the railing. It forced him to let go of my arm. I ducked under the deck and ran as fast as I could. He was chasing me. He started shooting so I ran for the trees. I hid under a fallen tree for an hour while I heard him calling for me. He told me if he found me he would kill me. And if I went to you, he would kill us both. He said he would make me watch while he did to you all the things you did and worse in the video. When I heard him far enough away, I ran back to the house. I hurried inside to grab my keys and purse and drove away as fast as I could."

Another sob shakes her, and she takes few deep breaths. I do too. My mind is racing. I need vengeance, but the asshole is already dead. The monster in me is close to the surface. I can't let him out. Not yet. I need to be calm for Keira. I need her to tell me the rest. Then I need to reassure her that she's safe. And that I'll never let her leave again.

"I couldn't risk going back to my apartment. I figured he knew where I lived. I took out as much cash as I could from the ATMs, and the bank the next morning. Then I paid cash for a motel room for two days. I knew I needed to get out of town, but I was trying to think of a way to tell you. To warn you.

"I didn't get the chance. Two days later I was run off the road. I was brought to the hospital as a Jane Doe and released a day later. A week after that, I was in a drive by shooting."

I quickly pick her up and pass her to Luca. Once she's

safely out of my arms, I let out the loudest roar I can. I scream at the top of my lungs. "Fuck!" I pull at my hair. I need the pain. How in the hell did I not know any of this? Why did I believe the note? Why didn't I go after her? How did I not see through Santo's lies?

It was Santo. Wasn't it? It's the only person it could have been.

I need confirmation.

I turn back to her. "What did the man look like?"

"What does it matter?" She extracts herself from Luca's arms. I can see the walls I tore down being built back up in her eyes. She thinks she still needs to protect me. She's going to try to run. Over my dead body. "It's over, I survived. I moved on. And I'd like to keep it that way." She says to me with bite, then turns to Luca and ask, "So can I go home now?"

I force Luca to ignore her with a glare his way. He puts his hands up and takes a step back. "Was he a few inches shorter than me? Dark hair. All black outfit?"

She looks between the two of us. Clearly not wanting to answer.

I storm over to her. The beast is loose, but he won't hurt her. I just pray he doesn't scare her too much. "Answer me." I growl.

"Yes." She whispers.

"Did he tell you a name?" She shakes her head no.

"If we show you a picture, would you recognize him?" I ask. Trying to keep my tone even. She nods.

I dig out my phone, and bring up a photo of him. It only takes a second for her eyes to widen. Then she visibly swallows the lump in her throat. Her arms go across her middle to hug herself.

She nods.

I throw the phone to Luca so he can see who it is. Then I prowl the last few steps to her. To her credit she doesn't flinch from my beast. There is no fear in her eyes. Not towards me anyway.

Luca must finally see the photo, because suddenly the room rings with a curse. "Son of a bitch!"

I latch my arms around Keira. Needing her scent in my nose. Her body close to mine.

With her held tight in my arms, we watch as Luca goes over to the bench and tosses it. It's not a light piece of furniture but he still manages to send it ten feet. Then he moves over to the bags and starts punching, kicking, and knocking it around. There is no rhythm or purposeful combination he throws. It's anger, rage, unadulterated hate that he is releasing.

As Luca's tantrum begins to ebb, Keira looks up at me. "Who is he?"

"He's dead." Hollers Luca.

Her eyebrows clench in thought as she looks to him, then back at me. "He was Don Bosco's Uncle and Consigliere. Until a few months ago, we didn't know he was a traitor, or that he was working with the Cartel and the Irish."

Keira gives me a confused look before confidently saying. "He wasn't working with the Irish."

"What?" Chills run down my spine.

"He wasn't working with the Irish. Killian and his father don't sanction business with the Cartel. They never have."

The hair on the back of neck stand up at the sound of his name. "How the fuck do you know the heir to the Irish Mob?"

Keira bites on her lip. Looking nervous as hell. "He's my fiancé."

My heart stops.

She said she hadn't been with anyone. That she only kissed one other man.

Killian. She's fucking kissed Killian Doyle.

Suddenly the floor shakes as the echoes of a loud blast rattle my ears. Luca takes off running towards the door. Keira takes a step away from me. Her arms back around her middle, holding herself protectively. "Sounds like he's here."

CHAPTER TWELVE

Keira

Val rushes up the stairs. I follow and try to rush ahead of him. If it's Killian who just set off that blast, which I suspect it is, he needs to see me and know I'm okay, so they'll stop firing.

I can't let Val or his family be hurt. If Killian has come in, guns blazing, then he must believe I am here against my will, which I was, sort of.

Shit.

Things are about to get weird, complicated, and probably more than a little violent.

The love I once had for Val, that I thought was gone, is still there. Still lingering. I don't know what that will mean for me and Killian. He's technically my fiancé, and for his plan to work, he still needs me.

We'll need to discuss things, if I can manage to keep everyone from shooting each other first. Killian is a good man. He knows I didn't leave Val willingly. He'll understand. I think.

As long as neither of the men I care for get hurt, we'll make things work. Somehow.

With Val not yet fully recovered, I am leaps and bounds faster than him, so once we are up the stairs, I dodge Val's arm as he tries to grab me and rush out the open front door.

I can see the front gate blown to smithereens. The guard shack beside it looks untouched. There is a guard on the ground I can barely see, but he is moving. Hopefully the blast didn't do any serious damage. Five all black SUVs are making their way up the driveway. When they get close to the house, they fan out around the third vehicle. I know instantly that one is where Killian will be.

All of his cars are bullet proof. I can hear the pings of the shots from the guards on the roof bouncing off the armor. Killian's men aren't returning fire. I keep running, not slowing even as Luca and Ricco yell for me to stop. I'm halfway to the vehicles when Val screams for a ceasefire. Silence follows, so I stop. I don't go any further. I don't want Val to think I'm choosing Killian by leaping into his car or arms. I just wanted the bullets to stop long enough for everyone to talk things out.

I feel a presence at my back. I don't need to turnaround to know its Val behind me. Thankfully he's smart enough not to touch me. I'm not sure how Killian would take it. I've never hidden anything from him. He knows Val was my first love. My only love. He knows the truth about why I had to leave him, even though I didn't want to.

The moment of silence ends as the driver's door of Killian's car opens. It's Grady. His right arm is down and hidden from view, as is most of his body. He's using the armored door as a shield in case they start shooting again. I hope they don't.

Grady gives me a smile as he asks, "you escaping, or are

we rescuing?"

I give a small laugh and smile back. "Neither."

The back door opens and Killian steps out. I can hear the guns being raised behind me, and feel the tension quickly escalate as Val's men and family come to learn just who stormed their compound.

"Killian." Growls Luca. I can hear the disbelief in his voice. It's understandable. Under normal circumstances Killian would never dare to attack the Italians. That's the shit his cousin likes to pull.

Killian straightens his suit jacket and strides confidently towards me. He doesn't flinch at the sight of the guns trained on him, nor does he have his own weapon out. "Evening Luca." He says with a chin lift towards the house. Then he turns his attention to Val. I hadn't noticed, but Val has moved closer. "You have something of mine. I came to get her back."

Val takes the last step towards me. Grabs my waist and pulls me behind him. "You aren't taking her." Val replies with venom.

Killian gives a smile. "You best let go of my fiancé."

Looking at Val, I see an entire catalog of emotions flicker in his eyes as his gaze remains locked with Killian's. He must find whatever he is looking for, because he turns to me. Giving his entire back to Killian. It's not disrespectful. In this instance it is a sign of trust. Trust that Killian won't shoot him in the back. It makes my heart thump louder for him. He doesn't know Killian, not personally. I do, and he's trusting me to know I don't associate with someone who would hurt him.

He moves closer to me, invading my space. His hands come up to cup my cheeks. His thumbs rubbing circles. "Do you love him?" He asks.

"We're engaged." I reply.

"Not my question." He says. Then he moves one hand from my cheek to the back of my neck and pulls my forehead to his. "Do. You. Love. Him?"

I chance a glance at Killian. He must see the indecision warring in my eyes. He gives me a nod before turning to Grady to give him a nod. It must be one of approval because Grady holsters his gun and moves out from behind the door.

Turning my attention back to Val, whose forehead is still pressed to mine. I lean my lips forward and kiss him. It's quick and innocent, but I needed him to not only hear my answer, but feel it. My voice is barely a whisper as I reply. "No."

I feel him relax against me. "You loved me once." It's a statement not a question. I nod anyway. "Could you love me again?" He hasn't let me go. I need a moment, but I don't want to step away from him. I don't want to lose this connection. So I close my eyes and take a few deep breathes. My engagement to Killian is important. A lot is riding on our union and the lies we've told and will need to tell.

I'm loyal to Killian. He's protected me for seven years. Given me a family.

But this is Val.

Tino. My Tino.

I hadn't let myself call him that in days. It didn't feel right if he wasn't mine.

All the memories we had, if they had never been tainted, if the cruel manipulations of Santo had never touched us, what would our lives have become? We had dreams of our future. But those were dreams for the people we once were.

We aren't those same people anymore. Are the new versions of us compatible? Could we step back into the relationship we once had, or would we need to start from scratch?

What would that even look like? We aren't kids anymore. He is in the Italian Mafia, brother of the Don, and I am the fiancé of the heir to the Irish Mob.

I open my eyes. Tino hasn't moved. I'm not sure he has even blinked. I see the strength in his gaze. The certainty. The love. It's the look. My look. The one reserved for me. It tells me all that his words can never say. He hasn't moved his hands. Mine are resting on his hips since I wasn't sure what to do with them, and felt awkward letting them hang at my sides.

Moving my hands up, I skim up his abs, feeling the hard planes through his shirt, and then grab onto it. Right over his heart. I pull his body closer to me.

"If ever I could love again. It would be with you." He brushes away the tears I didn't realize had fallen from my eyes.

"I'll make you love me again." He whispers. Then his lips are on me. Owning me. Pouring his emotions into every movement. When my lungs ache from lack of air, he pulls back, but doesn't let me go far. With more power in his words, and loud enough for Killian to hear, he continues. "I'll fight for an us. I'll breathe to cherish you. I'll awake each day to make you smile. I'll die to protect you. And I'll live to love you more and more each day, so never again will either of us need to feel the pain of being without the other."

Unable to contain the happiness in my heart, I climb him like a tree. Needing his lips on mine to seal his promise. Tino doesn't hesitate to lift me into his arms. Securing me to him. When I feel my lungs once again burn for air, I pull back, but only enough to rest my head on his chest. I've missed this. Missed his kisses. Missed the safety of his arms.

Killian did a great job protecting me. I'm alive because of him. A debt still owed. Even with his protection, I never felt as safe as I did in Tino's arms.

A throat clears beside us. Bursting my happy bubble.

Shit. Killian. I go to put my feet back on solid ground but Tino stops me. He holds me tighter, but does turn us so we can both look at Killian.

He gives me a smile, then turns to Tino, his gaze narrowed, his voice deep and menacing. "Hurt her, and I will spend a thousand nights torturing you before sending you to the gates of hell." I've seen Killian mad. Witnessed him step into boss mode and beat men into submission. Never have I heard this version of him. It sends a chill down my spine. In a good way. It lets me know that Killian is releasing me from my commitment. That he's happy for me. And that even though I am with Tino, a man in the opposing Mafia, he will still protect me.

Tino releases a hand from my ass and offers it to Killian. "Never." He promises.

Killian looks to me for a moment, I give him a smile. It's a small thank you compared to what I owe him. Smiling back, he grabs Tino's offered hand, and says "I believe it's past time our two families sat down."

Together, we turn to the house. Killian and Grady ahead of us, and Tino still holding me in his arms. Everyone's weapons are tucked away. I no longer see the snipers on the roof. The tension seems to be easing from everyone. Luca steps forward and holds his hand out to Killian then to Grady. "Agreed." Then as he turns to lead everyone inside, he add, "You also owe me a new gate."

Killian turns to me with a grin and a wink. It allows the rest of the tension and nerves to drain from my body. It leaves me feeling exhausted. Good thing I don't need to walk, and Tino feels just as content to keep me in his arms. I have a feeling it will be a while before he is ready to let me go.

Considering I have had limited physical contact with people for seven years, I am surprisingly okay with it.

Because it's Tino.

CHAPTER THIRTEEN

Val

We couldn't all fit into the Don's office, so we opted for the dining room. Violet, Livianna, and Milan are helping everyone settle by offering drinks, food and snacks. Killian and his second, Grady, are polite and patient as everyone bustles about.

Finally, when everyone has a drink and been offered food, Luca, who's seated at the head of the table, clears his throat to get everyone's attention. Immediately everyone silences and turns to him. Killian is across the table at the other head. Grady to his right, mirroring Massimo at Luca's right. Bosco has taken my usual seat to the left, so that Keira can sit down by Killian.

I don't want her to feel like she has to choose sides. We are gathered peacefully and I want it to remain that way. The Irish have been a thorn in our side for decades, but much like how Santo deceived us, I am starting to believe the Irish, or at least Killian may be in a similar situation.

"Keira, can you tell us how you came to know Killian. As

far as I know, you have no connection to the Irish family." Starts Luca.

She squirms in the seat beside me. Looking to Killian and Grady. Before she responds, Killian speaks to her softly. "Go ahead Cahira. I don't want you to have secrets from your family."

She nods but then asks, "what about you're..."

He reaches out to grasp her hand on the table. "I will share my bit after. I really do wish to work alongside the Caruso's. I won't hinder that trust by keeping unnecessary secrets from an ally."

Keira appears to give his hand another squeeze before she lets him go and grabs my hands and places them both in her lap. "As Tino already knows, Santo came to me and forced me to write a break-up note. He was going to kill me, but I escaped. He had told me he would make Tino pay if I ever told him or tried to get in touch with him." Her hands are shaking, so I grip them a bit tighter. "I didn't get out of town fast enough. He sent men after me. First it was a car accident, then a drive-by shooting. There were a bunch of small attacks that were too frequent to be coincidental. About six month later, I gathered the courage to try and approach Club Vivid. Tino had told me it was family owned, so I hoped if I went, I could find someone who could reach him for me."

Fuck, even without hearing it, I know this is the part she tells me about the scars on her back. I release her hands and grab her waist. I lift her onto my lap and tuck her in close to my chest. She leans against me.

"I was close. I could see the neon sign, when someone grabbed me. They pushed me into the alley. I tried to get away. There were two of them. I couldn't escape. They were trying to rip my clothes off. Told me I was a pretty little thing and they couldn't wait to feel me. I knew they were going to rape me, so I fought harder. They punched me and I think I blacked out for a minute, when I came to they had ripped my shirt off, but my pants were still on. One of the guys was still holding me. He had a knife. The second guy was on the phone. He was telling someone about my tattoo. Saying that they hadn't been told I was protected."

And she should have been. If she was ever in trouble with anyone in the family, that mark should have protected her, and had her brought to me.

"I'm not sure exactly what he was told, but when he hung up, he grab his knife and sliced through my tattoo, saying my protection was revoked. That I deserved everything I got for betraying the family. They cut me a few more times, until a group of guys heading to the club yelled at them to stop. The attackers ran off, and one of the guys gave me his shirt to cover up with. They offered to take me to the hospital but I didn't know if they could find me there. I went back to my crappy new apartment and patched myself up as best I could."

"I'm so sorry Keira. I'm so sorry I wasn't there for you. My mark should have protected you. Those men should have called me no matter what that other person on the phone said."

She nodded. "I stayed mostly in my apartment after that. I still had money from my parents, so I didn't need to work. I only left to get groceries. I wasn't attacked again, but I knew it wouldn't last. Then one day while heading home from the store, I spotted a guy bleeding on the side of the road. I stopped to help him." She looks at Killian and smiles. "It was Killian. I had no idea who he was, only that I needed to help. I brought him back to my place, patched him up, fed him, and let him rest. When he was feeling stronger he called

Grady to have him pick him up. Before he left he told me he owed me a blood debt, and handed me a card with his number on it. Told me to call if I ever needed anything."

She pauses so long, I wonder if she's able to continue on. Tears are streaming down her cheeks again.

Finally Killian picks up where she left off. "Two weeks later she reached out. Told me her apartment was broken into. I didn't ask questions. Grady and I hopped in a car and rushed to her. Brought her back to my apartment building, and promised to keep her safe. I knew there was something, or someone she was hiding from. A month later she trusted me enough to tell me about Val, and the attacks. I was never able to figure out who from your organization had threatened her or organized the attacks."

"Santo. He's dead now." I tell him. I want him to know the threat is gone.

He gives a nod of appreciation. "She's saved my life a total of three times, and she's become one of my closest friends in the process. I trust her. My men trust her."

Grady then adds, "They see her as a little sister. They protect her as one of our own." He turns to Keira. "Always. Even here. If you ever need us, we are a call away."

Keira smiles brightly. "Thank you Grady." And then to Killian, "Thank you."

"You saved me first." Replies Killian.

"So how did your protection turn into an engagement, was that a stipulation to the protection?" Asks Luca.

Fuck. I forgot about the engagement between them. The reminder makes me squeeze her tighter to me.

"No." Says Keira.

"Absolutely not. Keira has been under my protection for the last six years. The engagement was more of a mutual arrangement we came up with about a year ago." Killian

93

takes a breath and closes his eyes for a moment. "Succession in my family follows blood. Same as it does yours. My father is not a strong leader. He recognized this years ago and allowed the wrong men into positions of influence. One being my Uncle. He undermines my father wherever he can. He's made an underhanded deal with the Cartel. Only those closest to my Uncle and Cousin are meant to know about it. I suspected their treachery and have been working to remove them. They have a loyal following, and are technically blood.

"A little over a year ago, my father found out he is sick. Cancer. He doesn't have long left. It was never meant to be announced, but word has gotten around, and my cousin has been making a bid to supersede me as my father's successor. Without out right killing me, there isn't much he can do other than to spread lies. There is one secret that, if it got out, could turn the tables. Only three people currently know. Myself, Grady, and Keira."

Killian looks to each of us. Measuring us. Seeing if we are fit to know the secret.

"I'm sterile. I cannot have biological children. So I cannot continue a bloodline. With Keira knowing my secret, she agreed to marry me, to undergo secret in-vitro-fertilization so that my secret would never be found out, and the family had the heir they would need."

"Wow." Says Elena. Then turns to Keira. "You were willing to give up on finding someone just to help him."

Her answer shocks the room. Not me. Because it's how I've felt. "I had already found and lost the love of my life. I knew I would never find anything close to it again. So I agreed to Killian's proposal. Knowing he would keep me safe and do what he could to make me happy. He would never pressure me for more than I could give, and he was willing to accept that I would never love him. But would love any child we had."

"What about your brother? Couldn't he take the throne?" Elena asks.

Killian's face goes white. "He's dead."

"You had a brother?" Asks Luca.

"A twin. And as I said, he's dead."

"Strange. I didn't know Kansas was where you went when you died." Replies Elena with a smile. She loves to be a shit stirrer. I wish she would read the room. Now is not the time.

"Leave him out of this." Snarls Killian. He's on his feet. Looking ready to leap over the table and strangle her.

Elena gives a shrug. "I do not wish him harm. I only mentioned him, because he is of blood. Your blood. So a child of his would be included in the line of succession."

Killian sits back down. "That is inconsequential. He has no children."

"He has one, and another on the way." She responds.

"How do you know?" Asks Grady.

Elena pulls out her phone. She types for a minute before placing it on the table and sliding it towards Killian. I am able to sneak a glance at it before Killian picks it up. A man identical to Killian has his arm wrapped around a woman holding a child. His other hand cradles the small bump of her stomach.

"Where did you get this? Why do you have it?" Killian asks suspiciously.

Elena holds her hands up. Trying to show she isn't a threat. "I'm a hacker. I was the one to discover Santo's secrets. I found his connection to the Cartel, and through it, I found your cousin. Not knowing who we could trust, I dug further. It's why I trust you. I found no reason not to. Same with Keira. It's why I allowed her to be here before Val woke up and could vouch for her. While digging I found your brother. If you are wanting him to stay hidden, we need to do some work. I'm good, but not the best. If your Cousin gets someone better on his payroll, he could find him too."

"Can you do it? Can you hide him?" Killian asks. He looks to be sitting on the edge of his seat. Like his life hangs in the balance of her answer.

"Yes." She says.

Killian gives a nod.

Luca being the Don, pipes in. "Elena and Val will work to hide and protect your brother. As for our relationship going forward. What are you willing to offer in exchange for an alliance?"

"Your last two rats." The room goes quiet at Killian's declaration. We had all believed we had exterminated the last of them with the demise of Joseph. Before I can wrap my head around the news, Killian continues. "I know Santo was working with the Cartel. He infected my own ranks thanks to my cousin. Become my ally. Hide my brother, help me take down my cousin, I'll give you the two names and together we can take down the Cartel and their trafficking business."

Luca strokes his hand over his short beard as he takes a moment to think it over. It's a good plan, and it would give us an alliance with the two other powerhouses of the city. It could mean peace for us all.

"We will agree to help you. In every way we can, however without a blood bond or marriage between our families, the council will never allow a formal alliance and treaty. The most we could formally offer is a temporary truce."

"Not good enough." Says Grady. "If Killian is taking over, he will need his position to be on solid ground. That starts with an alliance."

"Val and Milan are the only family of high enough status to solidify a pact." Responds Luca. "We need one of their hands to bond the Russians. We have already a verbal agreement with them, and the council has approved it. With Val being reunited with Keira that would leave Milan to marry Ivan. I doubt very much you would want to propose that Val marry an Irish blood whilst being with Keira."

"Never." I shout. I shouldn't yell at my Don. But for Keira, I will go to war with him.

Killian waves his hand as though it's not a big deal. "Of course not." Turning to us. Killian looks to Keira first, then me. "I propose Val marry Keira."

"Okay, but I fail to see how that solves our dilemma of a marriage bond." Reminds Luca.

"Keira is recognized by my inner circle and my loyal men as a sister in our organization. Bound by our blood debt. As I said earlier my men are loyal to her even before our engagement. As a recognized member of my family, or the inner most circle of the Irish, would your council agree to it"

Holy shit. Could that work?

Please work.

Luca ponders for a moment, before turning to whisper to Massimo. After a minute, he turns and does the same with Bosco. "I believe we could get them to agree. However, I will not force the hand of my brother nor Keira. They have lost seven years together. I do not wish to force their hand only to find that the love they once had no longer exists."

I open my mouth to argue. Ready to declare my undying love for Keira, but Luca raises his hand to stop me. "I am not trying to deny your feelings brother. I want you both to think on it. Spend time together. Get to know one another again. In the meantime, we agree to a truce. We will work to further hide your brother, take down your cousin and eliminate the

Cartel from the city."

Luca and Killian both stand, and round the table to meet in the middle and shake on it.

CHAPTER FOURTEEN

Keira

Well, this is awkward.

Tino and I are sitting in a private study. Actually it may be his office. There is a modern looking gaming desk in the corner with three monitors mounted on a single stand. The rest of the room doesn't match the aesthetic. It's all rich mahogany bookshelves, and leather couches. Landscape paintings that probably cost more than my medical degree hang on three of the four walls. There isn't anything personal in the room except for the desk set-up. Knowing how much Tino loves computers, I'm betting it's his.

We've been sitting in silence for about five minutes. Tino is beside me. He's not making me sit on his lap at the moment, but we are touching from toe to hip. He hasn't said a word since we got in the room. We used to be able to sit in silence for hours at a time and it never felt weird, or necessary to fill the void.

Does he feel the same way about it now? Or is he anxious like me?

I've been avoiding looking at him, as I'm not sure what I'll see on his face.

I'm not sure what I am hoping to see on his face either. Taking a deep, fortifying breath, I gather up my courage and turn to look at him.

His face doesn't give much away. It's sort of blank. Not angry, or sad blank. More like peaceful blank. "Hi." I say.

Oh my god. Did I just say freaking hi! Shoot me. Someone put me out of my misery.

Tino laughs. It's sweet. Not condescending like my mind was fearing. "Hi." He says back. Then he leans forward and brushes a strand of hair away from my face, tucking it behind my ear. "I missed you."

I can't help the smile that crosses my face. "I missed you too." We fall back into silence. This time it feels less awkward, and only lasts two minutes.

"I don't want us feeling like we're walking on eggshells around each other." I nod. Same. "You can ask me anything you want. I'll answer as truthfully as I can. I also want you to know, you aren't a prisoner here. I'm sorry Luca and everyone made you feel that way." He blows out a breath, it makes the ruffled hair on his forehead flutter. "Luca knew I had been looking for you. He didn't want you to leave and risk me losing you again."

"You were looking for me?"

"Yeah." He looks nervous. "I hate it, that I didn't run after you back then. I was angry and Santo was keeping me busy with odd jobs. Looking back I think he did it so I didn't have time to look for you. By the time I could think straight, I figured it was too late to beg for your forgiveness. The night I missed you at the lake house, it was my initiation. The video you saw, was the first man I killed. It's how you become a made man in the family."

He pauses. I think he's waiting for me to freak out. Seven years ago, I may have. I'm not that same girl. And just like on the day Santo showed me the video, if he had reason to do it, a good and valid reason, then I can live with it. Considering, my hands are no longer clean, it would be hypocritical of me to hold this against him. I decide not to say anything. Instead, I reach forward and take his hands. Hoping he understands my silent request for him to continue.

He does. "A while ago, it was brought to the family's attention that Santo was a traitor, we had been blind to it for decades. We learned he was doing unsanctioned work with the Cartel, along with various other things. It was then that I started second guessing every interaction I had had with him. One being the morning after my initiation. I had called you to say I was finally on my way. When you didn't answer, I rushed to get there. I knew it wasn't like you to not answer, and I was scared one of our enemies had found you. When I got there, Santo was on the porch. He had the note you wrote. It was in your handwriting so I never questioned it. I was so angry at you. And at the time, I never would have thought Santo was capable of something like that. He was present when I asked permission from the Don to tattoo my mark on you, and to tell you about us. I thought I had his approval too."

He pulls one of his hands free from mine, to run it through his hair. "I recently discovered the reason why Santo ran you off. He needed me single. Needed me free to marry someone else. I came across a contract about a month back. Santo had promised my hand to a daughter of a Cartel Captain in Vegas. He had wanted to convince the Council to agree to an alliance and seal it with my marriage to that girl. With Luca having the contract to become Don, Santo knew getting the brother of the Don into a marriage would raise his position within the Cartel."

"What happened with the girl? Did you ever meet her?" I ask. From what I know about the Cartel from Killian, they can be ruthless, even to their own children. If her father is one of those men and wants someone to blame, he may blame the daughter. I don't know her, or know if she is innocent, but my heart goes out to her.

"I never met her. I only know a name. The contract was never signed by Don Bosco, or the Council, so it's worthless."

"Do you think the girl is in danger?" I can hear the urgency and distress in my own voice. I remember back when I was young, vulnerable. No one in my corner. Is that how she feels?

"Hey, babe, calm down." He pulls my arms so I'm forced to lean forward, and rock onto my knees. Grabbing my hips next, he pulls me and spins me so I'm on his lap. He rubs his hand up and down my arms. "I'll see what I can find on her. Between Elena and I, we should be able to find some information. If I think she's in danger, I can call the Don in Vegas. He owes me a favor."

"You would do that?" I ask. I hate feeling the need to ask. I never would have last time.

He presses a kiss to my temple. "I'd do anything for you."

"Would you streak naked down the street?" I tease. Tino smiles deviously. Then leans us forward and starts to pull his shirt up. An embarrassing squeak leaves my mouth when I see his abs poking out beneath the shirt. He pulls the shirt the rest of the way off, then tosses it across the room. My eyes roam up from his abs, to his pecs. My gaze locks on the lone tattoo on his chest. There are more on his arms, but only the one on his chest. My hand floats up to touch it. It's not a conscious move. I run my finger down the stem of the black rose. Right over my name. "You still have it."

Tino interlocks his fingers with mine and brings it to his lips and kisses each knuckle. Then brings it back to lay against his chest. "It never crossed my mind to remove it. It's part of me. Just like you are." Seeing his tattoo in pristine condition reminds me of my own mangled mark. Tino can read the disappointment on my face. "When you're ready. We can get you a new mark. If you want one."

There is no hesitation on my part. "Yes."

He laughs and pulls me close. "Good. And if you want to cover up the old one, or see if it can be fixed, there are a few amazing tattoo artists in the family that specialize in tattooing over scars." Emotions threaten to choke me. Instead of speaking I nod enthusiastically. I had looked into covering it a few years ago, but it hadn't felt right. Knowing I had Tino's permission, encouragement even, made me feel a thousand times better about doing it.

Getting us back on topic, I decide to start asking questions. "So you found the contract and decided to go looking for me?" It's a little disappointing he wasn't looking before then.

"No. Well, sort of." He huffs a bit and starts again. "There has rarely, if ever, been a day that has gone by that I haven't thought about you. Usually it was to wonder what you were doing. Curious if you had met someone else. Hoping you were happy, but also pissed to think you were settled down, when I couldn't move on. When the Santo shit happened, it made me think back to that day. I started to see it in a new light. Instead of wondering what you were up to, I began to question if he had you murdered, or sold off to the Cartel. Those thoughts brought me to my knees. I became obsessed with finding out what happened to you."

I listen intently as Tino tells me how he combed through

Santo's computer, phone, desk, files, car, and even gym locker. He left no stone unturned but couldn't find any details of what had happened to me, or why, aside from the marriage contract. So he turned to the web. Looking for me, running facial recognition. He said he got desperate and started combing for female doctors in my age range. When he found one that had a matched that also had a strangely vague and minimal background beyond six years ago, he allowed himself to hope.

"I was going to go to the hospital and see you. Figured if it was you, I would recognize you right away. The day I planned to go, was the day I was grabbed."

"Is that why Luca sent for me? Because he knew you were looking for me?"

"Sort of." Tino looks shy suddenly. Maybe even a little embarrassed. "I uh. I was going in and out of consciousness when they found me. I didn't remember it at the time, but Luca told me I kept saying that I needed Dr. Jones. He thought maybe you were the only one I trusted or something. So he sent his men to grab you. When I woke up, I didn't remember asking for you, or that I was looking for you. Hell, for a while, I couldn't even remember Luca's name. But every time I closed my eyes I thought of you. Not Doctor you, but Keira. My Keira, from years ago." Then he laughs again.

All I can do is smile. He thought of me. Wanted me even when his thoughts were a scrambled mess. My heart beats a bit faster.

"When my brain started to work again, I asked Luca about you. I saw that he was keeping you in the basement, but I couldn't figure out why. He wouldn't tell me. Just kept saying you needed to be here. When I saw you sparring with Massimo, it all made sense. Luca wanted me to figure it out on my own. He wanted to see if I would recognize you. Back in the day I had told him everything about you. Couldn't stop talking about you. He realize you were different. Knew we were both different and wanted to see if it made a difference, or if we still felt that we were meant to be."

I think I know, but I need to hear it. "And what did you decide?"

"I love you Keira." Holy shit! "I loved you then. I just never told you. I loved you even when I thought you left me and wanted you happy even when I was pissed as shit. I love you now, even knowing we have grown up and our lives have changed." He presses my hand back to his chest, and puts his other hand on mine, over my heart. "This is the same. My heart and soul still recognize you as my other half."

"Mine too." I push his hand off my so I can climb closer. I straddle his lap as I kiss him. Long and deep. Until we are both panting. Then I pull back and rest my cheek on his naked chest.

The silence is peaceful this time. Tranquil. It lulls me to sleep. Tino too. I feel his heartbeat steady and his breathes deepen below my face. My mind isn't racing. I'm not needing an adrenaline rush.

Until the nightmares hit.

CHAPTER FIFTEEN

Keira

"No. No. Tino, no." Logically I know I am stuck in a nightmare, that this isn't real.

A warm and gentle hand is caressing down my face. Saying words of encouragement to wake me up. I can't. What if reality is worse? What if I imagined finding Tino again? What if Santo or his guys found me this time?

"Killian!" I scream into the dream. He'll save me. He has to.

"Keira. Wake up." The voice is harsh, commanding, but not cruel. I can feel myself wanting to listen. "It's Tino, your Tino. I need you to wake up babe. You're crying is killing me."

"Tino?" I don't know if I say it aloud or not. My eyes are beginning to open, it's hard to focus. It feels like the dream is fighting to keep me in it.

I'm disoriented, so when I feel a hand rub down my back, right over my shoulder where my tattoo is, I panic. Not again. Don't hurt me again. I thrash and kick. "No. Don't touch me.

Not again. No. Tino!"

My arms swing wildly, I feel like I'm on top of someone. My body goes into fight mode. "Ow, fuck." Then there's a grunt followed by a loud thud. I scramble back from my attacker. My eyes finally open and focused.

I'm in the study. In the compound. I take a few deep breathes to calm myself further then look around the room. Tino is on the floor. He looks in pain.

Oh shit.

"Tino. Oh my god. I'm so sorry. Shit. Did I hurt you? Please tell me I didn't hurt you."

He rolls into a sitting position, one hand cupping his manhood. "I'm alright. How are you doing?" He asks as he struggles to get back on the couch. There is a significant bulge in his pants that I can't stop staring at. "You got to stop looking at me like that babe."

"Why?" I ask shyly. I thought we were back together. Wait are we technically together? Do we have a title?

"Cause I'm going to want to do something about it, but considering you just rammed my nuts up into my abdominal cavity, we're going to have to wait a bit. And dealing with sore balls is surprisingly worse to deal with when you have an erection."

"Oh." My cheeks flush at the mention of his erection. Then I focus on the other bit of what he said. "Shit. So I did hurt you?" I scoot closer. Then stop and back away. I want to go to him, but I also want to run and get him ice. "I'm so sorry. I was stuck in the dream. And I didn't know what was real. I'm sorry. I haven't had one in a long time. I don't know why I had one now."

"Babe. Come here." He says. I don't. In fact I shift a little further back. "Keira. I need to hold you. Please." The sincerity in his voice and eyes get to me. I crawl across the sofa so I am beside him but not on him. He pulls me closer and wraps his arm around my shoulder. Tugging my head in closer, so it's resting on him. "I'm not mad. I'm not hurt. Just a bit sore. It will pass in a minute. I'm more worried about you. It's been a long couple of days. I think you are feeling vulnerable." I nod. Not wanting to look at him or speak at the moment. I want to absorb his strength.

"What would make you feel better? Want me to make you some hot tea, or warm milk?" He asks, and I shake my head no. "Want to go to my room, we can take a hot shower, then cuddle in bed with a movie?" I shake my head no again. Do I ask for what I need? Will he find it weird that I want to fight right now? I was a pretty girlie girl back in the day. I still like make-up and pretty things, but I also like to feel the power of throwing a punch.

"How about some pancakes? Are chocolate chip still your favorite?"

I sit up a bit so I can see his face. Trying to make sure it wasn't a lucky guess. "You remembered?"

"Of course." He says as me moves to stand, before lifting me up to my feet.

Livianna and Massimo are in the kitchen when we get there. She is pulling ingredients out of the cupboards, while he is making a pot of coffee.

"Morning." Says Tino. They both turn and greet us back.

Tino pulls out a stool for me at the counter then pushes my shoulder. I follow his unsaid instructions and sit. He moves around to the other side. The kitchen is large enough for the three of them to move around without bumping into one another. I feel weird being the only one not helping. Standing, I move to the cupboards and start opening them, looking for plates.

After my second cupboard Livianna speaks up. "Left of

the sink." I move to the cupboard she suggested, sure enough, the plates and bowls are there. I take out enough for each of us. Then turn to look in the drawers for the silverware. I figure they are in a top drawer nearby. I must go in the wrong direction because without prompt Livianna says. "This one." Then proceeds to open a drawer next to her hip. She isn't even looking at me. In fact, she's dipped her head down. Almost like she's afraid. No that's not it. Ashamed. Why is she ashamed?

Massimo gives her a big smile then grabs her around the waist and pulls her in for a kiss. She turns to me with a smile. Her hands wringing the hem of her shirt. "Sorry. Everyone is used to my quirks. I forgot you aren't."

"What quirk?" I ask.

"The Jedi mind tricks she does. You know, the one where she becomes a human lie detector, or handing you things you didn't realize you needed." Pipes in Elena from the door. Her right hand is held at an unnatural angle behind her back, with Luca right behind her. Is he holding her hand? How cute.

"I did notice the lie detector thing. You also have this weird calming effect on people." Turning to Luca. "Is that why you had Livianna delivering my food and always trying to talk to me?"

"Yes." He replies quickly. I like that he doesn't hide his reasoning.

"Smart." I tell him. Tino brings over a stack of pancakes. The counter is large enough that we are all able to fit around it. Livianna brings a bowl of scrambled eggs, and Massimo has a platter of bacon. We all dig in.

About two minutes into eating, I catch Elena in the corner of my eye moving. It's then that realize she has one arm handcuffed to Luca. She keeps yanking it, causing him to knock the food off his fork and start again. Unable to help myself, I begin to laugh. I look around the room to see if anyone else notices. They do. But no once says a thing. Only Livianna seems affected by sneaking glances and giggling quietly to herself.

"Are the handcuffs a kinky thing, or a protection thing?"

Elena gives one hard yank, then seems to pick the lock in two seconds and free herself. "It's a caveman thing." She says, as she tries to stand.

Luca is quick to pull her down on his lap and reattach the cuff. "It's for protection. Elena seems to think it's funny to sneak out of the room while I'm sleeping and run off." He sounds disgruntled but there isn't any real heat in his words.

Elena throws her hands up in the air. "I wasn't running away. I was literally going for a run. Around the compound. I didn't leave. And I took my guards. What more do you want me to do? I told you I wouldn't run again." She says defensively.

"Even if you did. I would hunt you down. Which is what I had to do this morning, after I woke up alone, with no note or text and your shoes gone."

Bowing her head, and kissing his chin. "You looked so peaceful, and I know you haven't been sleeping much. I didn't want to wake you. I'm sorry. Next time I will wake you to tell you before I leave."

"Thank you." He seals it with a kiss to her lips.

"Possessive bastard." She grumbles.

"Yep." Luca gives her another kiss, then stands, and places her back on the chair he vacated. Turning to Tino and Massimo he asks if they are ready.

I give Tino a questioning look. I didn't realize he had to work today. Speaking of work, I wonder when I can go back to working in the hospital.

"Sorry babe. Council wants an update. We've got a call with them in an hour. You good to hang out with Elena and Liv?"

I give a nod. "Sure. No worries. Do your thing."

"Thanks babe. I'll come find you as soon as I'm done."

The three men leave the room, while we clean up the breakfast plates. Once that's done, Elena turns to give me her best Cheshire cat grin. "Let's get you in the ring." She doesn't let me respond before she's grabbing my arm and dragging me down into the basement. She stops at a door just before the gym. It's a locker room. Tossing me some clothes, she then turns and strips off her own. Okay then.

The three of us meet in the gym once we are all changed. We stretch in comfortable silence before I jump on the treadmill to warm-up. Elena does the same, while Livianna moves to do some yoga poses.

Once my blood is pumping, I turn off the machine. Elena copies. Moving to the ring, we wrap our hands and climb between the ropes.

"I've been curious to see how well we'll match up." Says Elena.

I give her a smile. I'm usually really confident when I go up against other females. Elena is different. I've heard the stories. She was raised by her single mother on the run. They were constantly fighting for their life against a team of hit-men. To protect themselves, Elena trained with a man named Ronan.

He sounds bad-ass so I'm sure her skills will give me a challenge.

"Let's see what you got." I tease.

I take a moment to observe her. We are similarly built so neither of us can use the other's size or weight against the other. And from what I have seen, we are both pretty nimble.

111

We start off slow. I can tell we are each trying to learn each other's fighting styles. I have found that she pays more focus to my typical weak spots. Ribs, kidneys, knees. All good places. She was trained by someone who knew she might be up against men she could take out, so she would need to take them down, or bend them over in pain while she escaped.

That's not the way I trained. I trained to take the punches until their arms weakened. Then attack. I was trained to stay within the ropes. There is no running or hiding from your opponent. No weapons aside from your hands and feet. I can see her beginning to tire. She thinks she has the upper hand. She's landed a few good hits. My ribs on the left side are screaming and I can feel blood on my eyebrow seeping down the side of my face.

I watch her feet. She is planting them, readying to land her final blow.

Or so she thinks.

She's wrong.

It's my turn to play.

I dodge under her swing, then kick out her legs. She falls to the mat. I go down too, sweeping her onto her stomach so I can get her body locked. She is completely at my mercy. It's then that the doors slam open.

Even without her tapping out, I know the fight is over now. Luca will have my head if I manager to make her lose consciousness.

That was one of the best fights I've had mentally. Reading and anticipating my opponent. It was a nice change. Men are far too predictable. Elena had some stereotypical moves, but overall she was a good mix of techniques.

Luca practically runs to us and jumps into the ring. He pushes me away from Elena. Not hard but I can tell it's a warning. Tino is right behind him, and grabs me as I stumble a step back. He growls. Literally growls at his brother.

Luca is running his hands over Elena looking for injuries. He won't find any. She'll be sore. I made sure not to break anything or make her bleed. Tomorrow though is a different story. She'll have a bruise on her cheek, rib and hip. Her knuckles could use some ice too.

"Relax caveman. She didn't hurt me." She says to Luca as she lets him fawn all over her.

"Never again. Swear to god." Elena just smirks at him and makes no promise.

She gives me a wink over his shoulder. It's like she's saying "we'll see about that". He picks her up and throws her over his shoulder. He climbs out of the ring and walks to the door without jostling her too much. I'm thinking he's done this a few times with her.

Just before they are out of sight, Elena calls out. "I know you were pulling your punches bitch. I'm going to want a rematch."

"No." Shouts Luca as he swats her ass. Livianna laughs as Massimo wraps her in his arms. Massimo must see something in her eye because he spins her and says, "No. Not happening. You're pregnant and it's taking every ounce of my control not to tie you to our bed for the next nine months. Don't push it."

"I wasn't going to get in the ring." She says innocently.

"Good." You can visually see his shoulders relax.

"I was going to ask for lessons."

And the tension is back. "No."

"Mass…"

"No."

"Mass." She grabs his face and kisses him to shut him up. "Just listen you Neanderthal. I know basic self-defense and a few special moves. And you've been teaching me more."

"And that's all you need. Even that much is unnecessary. You will never again be in danger. I won't allow it." He says it with such conviction.

"I know you are going to try big guy. But truth is, our city isn't safe. Not yet. Until then, I would feel better to get more training. I want to feel the confidence they do." She says nodding my way. "I want to know that when our baby is born, I can help protect them."

You can see the moment Massimo caves. His shoulders slump and then he gives a nod. "If it will make you feel better. Safer. I'll allow it."

"Allow it?" She teases.

"Don't push it." He growls before she kisses him again. Without tearing his lips from hers, he scoops her up into his arms. "You can learn technique, no contact. No more than thirty minutes a day. You will then relax with a bath." He continues spouting off demands as he prowls out the door as she waves to us over her should. Then it's just me and Tino.

CHAPTER SIXTEEN

Val

I grab her hand. Seeing her in the ring was both arousing and terrifying. Watching my girl in her element. The smile on her face. The sweat glistening off her. Seeing the muscles move beneath her soft curves. Damn.

I was hard the second I stepped into the room. Then the terror came and my raging libido died instantly. The realization that she fought, that she trained to do that because of me. Of my inability to take care of her. Of letting her go so easily before. Of allowing us both to be manipulated by Santo.

Never again.

I can and will protect her. From all outside threats, and even myself. I know I am just as much a caveman as my brother. I want to lock Keira away in an ivory tower with the only key in my possession. But she doesn't need that. Not truly. She has had too many decisions already forced on her in the name of keeping herself safe. I will guard her.

I will be the monster in the shadows keeping her safe,

while she saves one life at a time in the hospital, or beats a man into submission in the ring. I won't control her.

As long as she lets me come along for the journey.

Without saying a word, I take her hand and lead her out of the ring and into the hall. Actions speak louder than words. I know she is still hesitant about us. We aren't the same people we were. We don't know each other the way we once did. Though I am beginning to learn more. Begrudgingly, Killian has clued me into some of the finer points. Letting me know she craves touch even if she won't ask for it. She needs to be busy. She needs to be active.

My cock stirs. Not now dude.

He has a mind of his own. I swear he's sending me visions of ways we could keep her active and busy in bed. The hours of exercise we could be having. Fucker. Not yet. I need our girl to know I see her. That I see her as she is now. Not as the girl I once knew. She's still there, but she's grown up. And I need her to know that there isn't a damn thing wrong with that.

I manage to get my dick back under control by the time we reach my suite. I need her in my space. Need her to see she fits here with me. "Let's clean you up, then get you some ice." I say as I lead her into the bathroom.

I have the first aid kit open and ready on the counter. She pauses at the site of it. I had watched her on the security cameras going down to the basement with the girls. The moment I saw them descend the stairs, I figured they were headed to the gym.

I pick her up and place her on the counter. Then push her legs open so I can stand between them. I grab a clean washcloth, get it damp, and begin cleaning up her face. "What are you doing?" She asks seeming nervous.

"Cleaning you up babe."

"Why? Aren't you mad at me?"

I raise an eyebrow. "Why would I be mad?"

"Cause I fought with Elena. Because I'm not the girlie girl in dresses and heels that I once was."

I grab her face. Making sure to keep her eyes on me when I know she wants to shy away. She's waiting for the rejection. Not happening. She still has lingering doubts. "Never. You want to train, I'll spar with you. You want to keep competing." Her eyes grow wider. Yeah, she didn't tell me that fun fact. I had to find out from Killian, that my girl was an underground fighting champ. It stunned the shit out of me. But honestly. I fucking love it. I love that my girl found a passion. Something that made her feel strong again so I had time to get my head out of my ass and find her. "I'll be cheering the fucking loudest. You want to wear scrubs or sweats everyday including walking down the aisle, I'll still think you're the sexiest fucking woman in the world. I loved you Keira. Not because of the clothes you wore, or the perfect persona you tried to project. I saw you. I see you. I still love you."

"You love me? How, why? We don't know each other anymore."

Ah. So that's why she hasn't said it back to me. Why she still had reservations. No worries, I can be patient. "I know enough. Know you are smart, strong, passionate, devoted. Know how you drink your coffee with two sugars and a shit ton of French Vanilla creamer. Know you like pickles on your sandwiches. Jalapeños in your cottage cheese. You hate the taste of water. Bottled, tap, cold, warm, doesn't matter you hate it, but you drink it because you know it's what your body needs. Know you became a doctor despite everything Santo put you through because you made a promise to your parents." I stop for a moment, so I can take the half-step closer to her, closing the gap between us completely. My hand moves up to cup her cheek while the other goes around to pull her ass closer to me. "There are a few things I don't know."

I kiss her nose. "Like how your come tastes." Moving over to her left ear, I nip at it. "How you sound when I'm fucking you." I move over to her other ear and repeat. "If our daughter will look like you or a mix of us both." Then finally her lips. I kiss her long and deep. Pouring my heart and soul into it. Letting her feel my erection rubbing against the heat of her pussy. When she begins to grind against me, I know I need to pull back or risk going off in my pants. "I can't think of anymore at the moment but I'm sure there are hundreds. And I pray I'm lucky enough to get to spend the next fifty to sixty years with you, so I can find them all."

A tear slips from her eye. She wipes it before I can. It lingers on her finger. She stares at it entranced. "Until you came back, I hadn't cried in seven years." Her admission guts me.

I'm rendered speechless. I'm not sure I'm breathing. My Keira is a sensitive soul. She used to cry at commercials for wildlife preservation funding. "I thought it was because I was broken." She continues. "But after a few months I knew that wasn't true. I wasn't broken. It was my heart." Her teary eyes, move from looking at her hand, to staring in my eyes. Into my soul. "It was missing." I cup her cheeks and bring our foreheads together. "From the moment I met you, you held my heart. I couldn't cry, couldn't mourn because a part of me knew you still had my heart and you would keep it safe until you could return it to me."

I can't help but to smile. I kiss her. Putting every bit of my heart and soul into it. All my love. "Not giving it back." I announce. She looks confused. I kiss her again. "It's mine.

Just as mine is yours. Ain't giving it back. I'm keeping it."

Her cheeks turn crimson from her deep blush. "Okay."

"There was never anyone else. I already said it, but I feel the need to repeat it." She pulls back slightly. Her eyes crystal clear. "No one. Not a fuck, a blow job, or even a kiss. I've given women passing glances. Never lingering because I knew they could never measure up to you."

She launches herself into my arms. "Me too. Except I did kiss a few times, but only ever Killian." I give a growl. I'm not mad. My inner beast is possessive. There was no stopping it from escaping my mouth. "It didn't mean anything. I swear. Just a few kisses, hugs and hand holding. He slept in my bed a few times when the nightmares became too much. But I swear he was a gentleman. He only ever held me. Rubbed my back and brushed my hair. Made sure I could calm down and feel safe."

"Not going to lie. Part of me wants to punch him for touching you. The other part of me knows I owe him a debt that I'll never be able to repay. He kept you safe for me." Our kissing resumes. And it gets hot quickly. She grabs my shirt and pulls it over my head. When she reaches for my pants I have to stop her. "Not yet."

She pouts. Full on pushed her bottom lip out and pouts. "Don't make me wait any longer. I've already waited seven years."

"Soon. I swear. I want to take care of you first." I bring her bruised knuckles up to my mouth so she can see them and I can kiss them. "You and Elena beat the shit out of each other, and I can tell by the way you're leaning that you're favoring one side of your ribs. Once I get you in our bed, we aren't leaving for a long time, so I'm going to need you to get your strength up." She pouts and tries to pull me back in for a kiss. "Let me do this please."

"Okay." I fill the bath with cold water, then move to the closet. On the floor below the shelves of towels, soaps, and bubble bath I had stocked up, is an ice machine. With the way my girl fights, she's going to need frequent ice baths to soothe the aches and pains, and I plan to be the one to give them to her.

I go about scooping the ice and dropping it into the tub. I can hear Keira rustling behind me. "You have an ice machine in here?" She asks. I nod, as I continue my task.

"Got it installed this morning. Wanted to make sure I had everything I needed to take care of you." I finish placing the last scoop of ice and turn to her. "Fuck." Naked.

My Keira is naked. Not an ounce of hesitation or nerves is showing on her face. She holds herself straight and tall. Confident. Damn right she should be. She is a goddess. Curves in all the right placed, yet has a damn six pack. How that is possible, I don't know. Don't ask me. Her nipples are hard, rosy points, begging for me to lick, suck, and bite them.

I don't let my eyes wander lower. If I do, I won't be able to stop myself from picking her up and taking her against the door, the wall, on the floor, on the counter, in the shower, and the tub.

Tub! I spin to turn off the water before it overflows. I pull the drain to let a bit of water out so Keira can get in. I can't speak. My tongue is in knots, and I'm trying to keep my lips closed so I don't drool like a fool all over the floor.

I offer her my hand to help her step in, so she doesn't slip, then I back up while she sits to let her soak. I need to keep my distance for a moment while I calm my dick down. With my hands in my pockets, I move across the room, to lean up against the counter.

When we're both satisfied her aches have been soothed. I help her stand and move her to the shower. She had a good sweat going. I had intended to let her shower alone. My girl had other ideas. She pulls me in. Clothes and all.

I am powerless to stop her as she strips me down to my boxers. There is no missing the giant tent my dick has created. She gives me a smirk as she runs a single fingertip along its length. Then teases me further by turning around, moving her hair over one shoulder and sweetly asking me to wash her back.

Unable to help myself, I do her back, then wash and conditioner her hair too. She is making the sexist moans as I massage her scalp. My dick which was already rock hard, is now a steel pole. I swear it's never been this engorged or hard before. The little minx knows it too. She grinds her hot little ass all on it. Thank god she kept one layer of clothing on me. The bastard is still trying to escape its cloth prison. If we were both naked, I'd have my cock in her already.

While I was distracted with thoughts of my dick, Keira somehow manages to turn around and drop to her knees. Her hands make quick work of dragging down my boxers. "Keira." I whisper. No, it's not a whisper. It's a moan. A plea. She is too gorgeous to resist like this. On her knees, eyes filled with lust, and her tiny fingers skimming my cock.

I try to grab her and get her to stand. She waves me off. "You're right. I am a bit sore." I nod in acknowledgment and attempt to get her to stand again. "I'm not up for anything more, but I want this. I wanted it then, and I really fucking want it now." Then her hand tightens around the base of my dick. Her tongue swirling over the head. Lapping at my pre-come that is continuing to leak out.

Her mouth is sinful. Taking me deep. Brushing her tongue on the other side with each back and forth motion she makes. Every few passes, she takes him completely out, and licks him. Going up one side and down the next. Then she teases the sensitive vein that runs along the base. I

I see stars. Her mouth and tongue move in random patterns, exploring what she likes and how I respond. I like knowing I'm the first. I love knowing she feels comfortable and confident enough to take what she wants and play me like a fucking fiddle.

Moving back to the head, she takes me deep. My tip hitting the back of her throat. She swallows around it and takes it a bit deeper. I'm done. Holy shit.

"Keira." I moan again. I can't talk. It's hard to focus as I hold back my orgasm. "Babe. Pull back."

She hums around my cock and I swear again. "Seriously babe, I'm about to blow."

She pulls back with an audible pop. "I know. I want to taste you."

"You want to…" My words are cut off as all my blood rushes to my cock as she pushes her head all the way down. Her nose brushing against the sensitive skin above my groin. I explode. There was no holding it back any longer. She drinks it down. Every last drop and continues to hum her approval as she does. She continues to suck well past when he's gone soft, to the point I start to harden again.

This time, when I bend to scoop her up, she lets me. The giant grin on her face only getting bigger as I pull her mouth to mine. I can taste myself on her tongue and I don't give a fuck.

After ravishing her mouth. I push her back against the wall of the shower. I drop her legs to the ground and only pull back once I'm sure she is steady on her feet. Then it's my turn to drop to my knees. I spread her legs wider. It's not enough. Pushing my shoulders between her legs so they are resting on me, I rise a few inches, her feet are off the ground, one hand goes to the tile, the other to my hair.

"What are you doing?" She asks. Her voice sounding stunned yet lust filled.

"Tasting you." I say as I press me face forward and give her a long lick. "Fucking delicious." I growl against her skin as I continue to feast.

She is soaking wet, and getting wetter. I want to stuff my fingers deep into her, but the monsters voice in my head says no. He wants our cock to be the first thing to breach her canal. Instead, I use my hands to spread her lower lips and get my face in deeper. I latch onto her clit and suck hard. Her hand pulls my hair. Her scream of ecstasy echoing throughout the room.

I keep her in place for another few minutes, softly licking her through the last of the aftershocks. When I'm positive I have rung the last drop of energy from her, I place her feet back on the ground and stand. I don't let her go. I can feel the unsteadiness of her legs. She is exhausted. I turn off the water, grab us two towels and take her to bed. I dry us both off as best I can, before I tuck her under the covers and climb in beside her.

She turns instantly and latches herself onto me. One arm around my chest, and a leg up over mine. "Sleep sweetheart. I'm never leaving again." I promise as I kiss her temple, and close my eyes.

CHAPTER SEVENTEEN

Keira

I wake with a smile on my face. My body feels sated, my mind calm. It's an amazing euphoria I've never felt before. I want more. Rolling over, I stretch my arm out, hoping to feel him. I don't. I feel only cold sheets. Sitting up, I scan the room and look for him. He's not here. Slipping out of the bed, I creep to the bathroom, the door is partially closed. Maybe he is in there, showering again. I could go for a repeat.

The room is empty. I try not to hide my disappointment. Fuck it. He's not here to see it. I let my irritation fly, and stomp into the room after slamming the door shut to do my morning routine.

By the time I'm done, my mood has calmed. I'm sure Tino is around somewhere. There has to be a valid reason why I didn't wake up next to him.

Sure enough, when I open the door, Tino is there. Sitting on the bed with a tray of breakfast. "Morning beautiful."

The smile I woke up with returns. He didn't leave me. "Hi handsome."

"Come here." I'm still naked as I step in-between his legs. It's a weird dichotomy having me naked, and him fully dressed. I don't hate it. It makes me feel empowered. His arms band around my waist, and he pulls me closer. Tucking his head into my stomach like he used to do. The position familiar and alien at the same time. By instinct, my hands go to his hair and being to massage. "I've got a day full of meetings." He says when he finally raises his head. I nod sadly. Knowing I'll be stuck here again all day. "I was wondering..." He kisses my belly then stands, all while keeping his hands on me. "Would you like to work at the hospital today?"

"What really?" I can't help but get excited. "Yes. No. Wait. I can't. They've probably let me go by now. I haven't been there in weeks and I didn't get a chance to tell them I needed leave." Damn. I wonder how quick I can get a new job. Or maybe I can set-up my own practice. Hmm.

"Babe. Did no one tell you?" He looks thoroughly confused, which only confuses me more.

"Tell me what?"

"We own the hospital. It's a Caruso owned business. Luca gave notice of your absence the day they took you from the parking lot."

"He did?" I ask. Did someone tell me? I can't remember. Maybe it sound familiar. Honest, so much has happened the last few weeks, I can't keep it all straight.

He leans down to kiss me. "Yeah babe. Your job will always be safe. You can go in and work part of a day, or a full day, it's your choice. We can talk tonight about what kind of schedule you want to have there." I open my mouth to argue. I don't want him interfering with my job. I worked hard to do it on my own. Before I can say anything, he continues. "Please let me do this. It's the only thing I ask, is that I get some say in the schedule. I don't want to control you. I want to make sure we get to spend time together. Lots of time."

Okay that I can understand. "Fine. But…" He eyes me skeptically, no doubt curious what I am going to ask for. "I want you to help me get my license transferred over to my real name. I want me back."

Tino smiles brightly at me. "Absolutely."

We eat breakfast together, before saying good-bye. An hour later I arrive to utter chaos in the ER. I don't think I just jump into action. There was a three car pileup on the expressway, and several ambulances had just arrived with injured passengers.

By the end of my ten hour day, I am exhausted. I had only intended to go in for a few hours to get back in the swing, but once I was there, I couldn't get myself to leave. The entire drive home, all I can think of is getting into an ice bath in Tino's room.

That plan is quickly ruined when I pull down the road that leads to the gates to the compound. I spot Killian and Grady in a standoff with two other men at the gate entrance. I don't recognize the two men as being from the Italian side. They either don't care or don't hear my car approaching. I keep driving down the road until my car is out of sight. I park and use the shadows to creep back to the confrontation. When I'm close enough to hear their voices, I recognize their accents. It's faint but there. Russian.

I don't like that Killian has a gun aimed at him, even with his own pointed back. And where the fuck are the Italians. How is it that this is their compound, and yet two other mafias are in a stand-off at their front gate without them noticing?

Fuckers. Guess I'll fix this shit. Moving quickly, and staying in the shadows, I get close to the Russians. Seeing the one has his trigger finger looking itchy. I decide to go for him first. Leaping out as quietly as I can, I get on his back with his weapon hand bent behind him in and uncomfortable angle. The pain brings him to his knees and weakens his grip so I can pry the gun loose. "Move and I'll brake your wrist." I growl into his ear. Pulling my new weapon up and pointing it at the second Russian, I tell him to drop the gun.

In my periphery I spot Killian putting his weapon away and stepping forward. Grady moves with him, but keeps his gun pointed at the man. They get to my side, just as Tino, Luca, and Elena come barreling down the driveway on a golf cart.

"Damn. Did we miss it?" Asks Elena.

"Nothing to miss." I say. "These assholes were just leaving." I pull on the arm of the man I'm holding. He rises to his feet. To his credit he doesn't make a sound.

"Nyet." Says the other, as he tucks his gun away." We have business to discuss."

"Funny." Says Killian as he crosses his arms over his chest. "So do we."

"Gentlemen." Jumps in Luca. "Our three families have a common enemy. I believe it is time we join forces to take back our city." Then Luca gestures towards the house. "Please, come to the house, let us discuss this together."

Ivan is silent and stoic for a moment before he gives a nod and tucks away his weapon. Only then, do I release my captive and hand him back his gun.

His eyes trail up and down my body appreciatively. I don't let him see a reaction. I know he is sizing me up. "Not bad." He finally says, then turns with his boss to head to the house.

CHAPTER EIGHTEEN
Val

I can already tell this meeting with be interesting. We hadn't anticipated that when we called Killian to come over and discuss the proposed alliance, that Ivan would be making a surprise visit to also discuss his alliance with us. No matter. Luca, Massimo, Bosco, dad and I have spent all day ironing out the details on our end. We are prepared, as long as no one starts shooting. Elena has her gun on her, and I'm a little terrified she's feeling trigger happy.

Keira is seated next to me on the couch in the living-room. Once again the office was too small, and the dining room table felt too formal for discussions between friends. She must be exhausted. I want to send her up to our room, but know that she will want to be here for this meeting.

"Ivan, to catch you up to speed, Killian will be taking over for his father in the coming months. His position is being opposed by his cousin. He came to us to seek out an alliance to strengthen his position. We have found the offer to be mutually beneficial, as well as preferable to a war with the cousin if he is to gain power."

Ivan turns to Killian. "I hate your fucking cousin."

Grady barks a laugh from the corner. It's amazing to see the three families having such similar customs. Massimo is also in a corner, while the Russian's second has taken up sentry duty beside the open doorway. Each position has a different tactical advantage.

Killian smiles back at Ivan. "We share the sentiment."

"So what of this alliance, does it affect the proposal we have shaken on?" Asks Ivan.

Luca shakes his head. "The only effect it has is that it takes Val out of the equation. The alliance to the Irish has been agreed upon by our Council, pending the union of Val and Keira."

Ivan's eyes wonder over to us. His eyes flick closely over Keira. "Cahira, the warrior. I have heard many things about you."

"You know of me?" She asks.

"Yes. You recently took down one of my best men. Bruno. It's because of you that they have added trainings to their schedules." He replies.

"Oh, I'm not sure that is a bad thing, so I'm not going to apologize." Ivan leans forward, the ghost of a smile on his lips.

"Don't apologize, it was a valuable lesson to my men. One I do not think they will forget for some time." He pauses a moment. "You are not of Irish blood. Are you sure the union is sufficient?"

A growl rips from my throat. "Of course it is." I bark.

"Ah, you are in love with the warrior." He states.

"Yes."

Ivan does not look satisfied. Killian must sense it too. "I owe Keira a blood debt. Three actually. She has been under my protection for years. My loyal men count her as family. They will protect her as family."

The answer seems to satisfy Ivan. He reclines back into his seat, and kicks a leg up to rest one ankle on the opposing knee.

"Val, Keira, you have three months to make your union official." I nod, then grab Keira's hand and place a kiss on the back of it. She has been silent throughout the meeting. I'm not sure if it's because she is tired, or if this is linked to some lingering doubt about us.

Milan enters the room, followed by Violet. Milan moves gracefully around the room, handing out drinks to those that want one. When her tray is empty, she turns to leave. But Luca calls her back as he rises from his seat.

"Milan," he says as he places a hand behind her back and escorts her across the room. "I would like for you to meet Ivan Vasiliev. Your future husband." He stops a few feet before him and takes a step back from Milan.

She looks older than her fifteen years. I'm willing to bet she ran to change when she heard her future husband was here. She must want to make an impression on him. Good for her.

Ivan does not move at first. His eyes never leaving her face. She maintains eye contact with Ivan. She is poised. Refined. A model of elegance. It is exactly as her mother trained her to be.

Only thing she couldn't train her to do was how to think like her. And thank god she couldn't. Milan may very well be the smartest person in the room. She grew up as the Don's daughter. He shielded her from the gore, but not the challenges and drama. Her mother trained her to be seen when needed, and how to fade into the background the rest of the time. Her mother had meant it as a means to please her future husband. Milan has twisted it. She knows as many secrets as Elena, has the respect of the men who followed her father, understands politics as Luca does, and now with the help of Luna, Elena, and I she is learning computers, in addition to speaking four languages. Russian not yet one of them, but I wouldn't put it past her to master it by year's end.

Finally Ivan stands. Instead of moving towards Milan, he curls his finger upwards. She scowls at him but moves forward at his silent command. When she is within reach, he takes her left hand, and without a word places a bracelet on it.

Milan looks from it to him, to Luca, and back to it.

He does not speak to Milan, but looks at her as he speaks to Luca. "We will wed one week after her eighteenth birthday." Milan is polite enough not to scowl at him, but you can see her bite her inner cheek. Then Ivan turns to her and says, "I cannot promise you flowers or romance. I may never grow to love you, or even care for you." Now she's scowling. "But I will honor our vows. You will be safe. You will bare our children. And I will try not to make you miserable." Milan snorts at that. Then he brushes the hair from her face and tucks it behind her ear. A light blush blooms across her cheeks. Then he leans in and whispers something to her.

At first her mouth drops. Then she pulls back and slaps him hard across the cheek. When his hand comes up to rub at the offending skin, she takes the opportunity to bring her knee up to his balls before storming from the room. Ivan's second laughs. "She will fit in just fine boss." Ivan stares at the door Milan vanished through and gives a nod.

CHAPTER NINETEEN

Keira

The days pass quickly. I stay busy at the hospital, and Tino remains locked in meetings with the Russian and Irish. In our little downtime together, we fool around, but never going all the way. It is maddening. When Tino is not in meetings, he is working to erase all digital footprints of Killian's brother. He knows how important Killian is to me, so keeping his brother safe is equally as important to me.

Plans are slow going. Or at least that's what I am to believe, until I am called into Luca's office. Tino looks rabid in the corner and is being held back by Massimo, Ricco, and Mario. Killian is standing across the room with Ivan and Grady holding him back. I'm not sure what I'm walking into, but I know instantly I am somehow involved

"You don't know her like I do. She will want to do it." Yells Killian to Tino.

"Over my dead body!" He screams back.

"I can arrange that." Shouts back Killian.

"What the hell is going on?" I holler louder than them all.

Killian is the first to speak. "Val is trying to keep you locked away like a prisoner."

"That is not what I meant and you know it." Retorts Tino. "I said it's too dangerous. I won't risk her." I can see Tino is ready to lose his shit. He told me about the monster he unleashed during his initiation. The same one that Santo used to his advantage for months, until Tino could lock away his emotions and bury the beast.

He doesn't want to be that again. He thinks it will scare me to see him out of control. His monster doesn't scare me, because he's my monster, and no matter what he does, he has a code that we won't break. No women, no children, and no innocents.

I take a few steps towards him. Making sure he locks eyes with me and keeps them there. "Tino. Sweetheart. What don't you want me to do?"

He pulls free of those holding him and grabs me. Pulling me in tight. Nearly too tight. It's a little hard to breathe but I won't complain. He needs this. Needs me. The room grows quiet.

Ivan is the one to break the silence a few minutes later. "We have all doubled our patrols and street forces, and made kidnapping new victims nearly impossible in the bars and clubs in town. Now we are learning that the Cartel has turned to the underground to hunt. The underground?

Oh…

Realization dawns on me. The fights. I think back to all the beautiful woman adorned in tiny, skin tight dresses and heels looking for a man to take them home, or already on the arm of a man who's looking to show his prized woman off.

Drugs can sometimes run rampant in the underground, and the security is there more for running interference if the cops or feds try to show up. It's a self-policed event. Killian hosted the events I went to, so I never had to worry.

But there are others. Ones run by the street gangs. Ones I have been invited to but always turned down. Killian chimes in next. "You received an invitation."

"But we know it's a set up." Mumbles Tino into my hair, before lifting his head. "They will go after Keira. I won't allow it. I'm not sacrificing her.

"Shh..." I whisper, trying to soothe my Tino, my beast.

"If I go... I try to start but Tino growls. Using my fingers to comb through his hair and massage his head, I shush him again. "If. If, I were to go. What would be the plan?"

"Gain an invitation, bring Killian and Grady there with you. This shouldn't cause an issue since they've been seen with you at all your previous fights." Says Luca.

"The Cousin would go for Killian, and the assumption is that the Cartel would try to take you, Keira." Adds Grady.

"All of you would have undercover protection in the form of my men. No one outside our inner circles know of our alliance. They won't think twice about my men being there, as I have several fighters in my ranks that make the rounds through the underground circuit and they always bring an entourage of friends and family with them. I'll be stacking those groups with my trusted men." Comments Ivan.

"Val and Elena would hack the cameras in and around the area to monitor everyone's comings and goings. Killian, Grady, and Keira would all wear trackers that Val and Elena will actively monitor. Goal would be to stop any kidnapping of you before they are able to get you out of the building. If they do manage it though, we will have two dozen vehicles and motorcycles stationed in intervals on the surrounding roads, to be able to follow and intercept no matter what route they take." Continues Luca.

"Word on the street is that the Cartel wants Keira alive to sell her. And the cousin wants to make a show of killing his cousin. He wants to make a statement. A proclamation. So he will not wait to hurt him. He will want to draw blood in the warehouse. But, he will keep him alive to suffer for a while." Says Ivan.

Tino continues to adamantly be against the plan, as he continues to shake his head in my arms and mumble the word no. I've also heard him quietly threatening to lock me in the dungeon.

"Can everyone clear the room for a minute?" I ask.

No one complains, or speaks again as they leave. When the door shuts behind them, I use my hands in Tino's hair to pull his head back so I can see him properly. "What are you afraid of?"

"We almost lost Liv. It was the same plan." His voice is strong, but his eyes are glazed with a mix of fear and anger. "I was already taken at the time. I was beaten, tortured. You saw the aftermath. They were brutal, efficient. And then they sacrificed Liv thinking they could keep her safe and find me in the process." His voice breaks a little but he continues. "They almost failed. It was too close. Liv had to fight. She had to kill a man with a piece of broken mirror in order to fend off his attack. And that was just one man. I know you are strong. You're a warrior. But I can't risk you. I lost you once. I can't go through that again."

I hear him. I do. I understood every word he said and I don't want to lose him either. "Tino, what if I told you I need to do this?" He shakes his head no. "Yes." I say. "After Santo ran me out of your life, I swore I would never be weak again. That I wouldn't let anyone take me from my family or endanger them if there was something I can do to help. You are my family, and so is Killian. Both of your families are threatened. I need to do this." I place a kiss on his lips, then tuck my head to his chest so I can feel his heart beating. "I have faith in our families to keep me safe."

"But what if..." He starts, but can't finish his sentence. It's okay. I know what he is going to say.

"If something bad happens, if something goes wrong, you will find me."

He refuses to listen. He keeps shaking his head. "No. I can't risk you."

CHAPTER TWENTY

Val

I need to show her what she means to me. That I can't risk her. I need her.

Keeping her tight to me, with one hand under her ass, and the other behind her back, I stand and carry her upstairs. "Where are we going?"

I don't answer her. When I get to my room, I carry her inside and drop her unceremoniously on the bed. Then I turn and go back to the door. I shut it, lock it, and place the chair from my desk under the doorknob. I don't want to be disturbed for any reason.

Prowling back to her, I see my girl hasn't moved other than to sit up on her elbows so she can watch me move around the room. Part of me realizes I should be making this special. I should be showering her in flowers and chocolate. Popping a bottle of champagne and toasting to us. There should be music and dim lights.

I don't have any of it, and in this moment I don't want any of it. They are all distractions. I want only her. Need only her. The heat in her eyes tells me she feels the same. Standing at the edge of the bed, I grab her ankles and use them to pull her to me. I take a breath, the beast in me wants to take her, claim her, rip her clothes to fucking shreds and own her. I won't. Can't. I'm going to savor every second I have her, for now until forever.

Grabbing hold of the little control I have over myself, I slowly peel her shirt off. The swell of her gorgeous breasts bouncy behind the pink lace bra with each of her breathes. Reaching around behind her, Keira undoes the clasp for me. She keeps her eyes locked on mine as she does.

With the garment on the floor, I move to her pants. Slowly I drag them down her legs, peppering her skin as I go. I leave a trail of goosebumps that makes my dick grow harder. She is so responsive to my touch.

Once I have her naked, I lift her to the center of the bed, then crawl off so I can remove my own. In a flash every stitch of clothing is at my feet, and I'm back on the bed with her. Kissing her. Holding her. Letting her feel me from the tips of her toes, to the top of her head. I want her to feel consumed by me. Her mouth is sinful. I could spend all day kissing her lips. With great effort, I pull away so I can move down her body to my next destination. I lick, suck, and bite a path to her dusky nipples. They are hard points that look almost painful.

I take one in my mouth. Warming it with my tongue, before giving it a little bite then flick. She moans loudly. "Tino." Her hands grabbing at my hair. Pushing me down further. I open my mouth wide and take as much of her breast into my mouth as I can. Her back arches off the bed. I move to its twin and repeat the process.

Keira's warm center is pressed against my stomach. Leaving a trail of her wetness. It reminds me that I have another place I need to kiss before I finally make her mine. I shuffle the rest of the way down her body. Putting my face flush with her pussy. Hooking each arm around a thigh, I spread her open for me. I take a long lick from back to front. Moaning at the taste of her sweet ambrosia. "Fuck." I groan. It's only the second time I have ever had my mouth on a woman. I have nothing to compare it to, but I know without a doubt, she tastes the best. The more she moans and rocks her pussy against my face, the more confident I grow in my actions.

"Don't stop." I do as she says. In this moment she owns me. I lick and suck and bring her to the edge a couple of times. She's begging me for release. Pleading with me. It's not enough. I need to hear her screaming my name in ecstasy, and I need her to do it with her come coating my cock. But first I need to make sure she is ready. Need her wet enough to take me so I don't hurt her more than necessary. I take her clit into my mouth and suck hard. I've done it before and felt how much it made her tense and moan, she liked it, but I pulled back before bringing her over the edge. This time I do. I keep my suction strong and I flick the buddy with my tongue. Her back arches off the bed, her whole body tenses. She doesn't even breathe for a moment. Then I feel it, the sweet cream of her release dripping down my chin and she yells my name for the entire compound to hear.

I trail kisses back up her body as she comes back down to earth. "Keira." I say, just barely a whisper. She looks completely blissed out. The beast in me is pounding his chest. Proud as hell, we did that to our girl. Her eyes flutter open, and take a moment to focus. "I love you Keira. I'm never letting you go again. I will fight for you. For us."

Settling my hips between her thighs, lining up my cock, I kiss her again. I pull back so I can see the expression on her face as I make her mine. Dipping my hips, my cock breeches her tight entrance. Keira's arms go around my neck and pulls my lips back to hers. I pause to let her adjust to me and to focus her lips. When she pulls back, there is a shimmer of tears glistening in the corners of her eyes. "I love you Tino. I have always loved you. Take me. Fuck me."

I press another inch in. "This is making love, not fucking." I mumble as I punch through her virginity and encase my entire cock in her warm pussy. "Holy fuck." I shout. It feels so good. I knew it would feel amazing, but holy shit.

The pain of Keira's nails digging into my shoulders pulls me from my lust filled haze. Looking down at her face, her jaw is tight and her eyes are closed. "Fuck Keira, I'm so sorry. I heard that it hurts. I'm sorry. I thought if I went quick it would be like ripping a Band-Aid off. Shit. Do you want me to pull out? We can stop."

"No." Then she shakes her head. "Yes."

"Ok, I'll stop, I'm sorry." I raise up on my arms further and begin to inch out. I go slow this time not wanting to hurt her again. Halfway out, she clenches around me and moans. I drop my head to her shoulder and wait it out. I'm so close to coming. She feels so, good but I won't take pleasure while she's in pain.

Her ankles move to press into my ass. She's pulling me back in. "Keira?"

"Don't stop. Keep going. Feels so good now." I move forward an inch to test her reaction. I need to be sure. She moans and arches into me so I sink in further. "Yes! Keep going."

That's all I needed to hear. I thrust in and out in a slow but steady rhythm. Each time she feels restless beneath me I pick up the speed, until I am pounding into her. The headboard is slamming into the wall. Probable leaving a dent, and I don't care. "Harder." She cries.

"Fuck baby, you're close aren't you. You're gripping me so tight."

"Yes." She says. "Right there, Tino. Right there."

"Hang onto me baby." She's so close, but there is another position I want to try first. With her arms and legs wrapped around me, I lift her up and rock back onto my heels. The angle hits different, I feel deeper. "Fuck, babe, keep clenching me."

Two more thrusts and she's screaming her release. "TINO!" I'm a stroke behind her. My come spurting deep inside of her. My body wants to collapse from exhaustion. I feel my energy draining. Slowly I pull out of her, and lay her on the bed. I crawl in beside and wrap my arms around her. "I love you Keira."

"I love you Tino." She says back before she drifts off to sleep.

I wake her three more times in the night to have her. The sun was coming up when I finally let her get some sleep. I watched for a while. Unwilling to tear my eyes from her body, until I could no longer keep my lids open.

Hours later, I feel refreshed. I stretch and reach out my arm for Keira. She isn't there. The bed is empty. I attempt to roll over to see if she's in the bathroom, but my arm is stuck. What the fuck? Looking up to the headboard, I see my wrist shackled in a handcuff.

I scoot myself up so I can try to undo it. I don't have anything to pick it with. Turning to the bedside table, I search for a key. There isn't one. But there is a note.

My hands shakes and I reach for it. It's Keira's handwriting. "I'll come back to you. I promise."

"No!" I roar. Fuck. Fuck. Fuck.

I bang and slam the headboard against the wall until the wood cracks. It might have been minutes, or it might have been hours. The red ring of rage in my vision is clouding my perception of time.

When my cuffs are finally free, I stomp out of the room, not even stopping to put on a pair of shorts. Butt ass naked, I storm through the house to Luca's office. Elena and the rest of the family are there.

Except for Keira.

Luca approaches me as though approaching a wild animal. Hands up to show he's not a threat. Like hell he isn't. If he didn't help her leave, then he sure as fuck didn't stop her, and that's just as bad.

When he's close enough for me to reach, I pull back and swing. The punch landing on his cheek. He doesn't swing back. He takes it. Knowing he fucked up.

"I swear brother, she will be save."

Putting my face an inch from his, "If she dies, I will reign hell on this city. Nowhere will be safe. And there may not be anything left for you to rule once I'm done." Luca knows full well how serious I am.

Then I turn and storm out before my beast decides to play.

CHAPTER TWENTY-ONE

Keira

The guilt of leaving Tino weighs heavily on me. But I needed to do this. I need this fight with the Cartel to end. For him, and for Killian. There is already too much blood on the streets, too much chaos. I see it every day in the emergency room.

If something doesn't change soon, an all-out War will happen on the streets of Chicago. No one will be safe.

Tino says this isn't my fight. It is. I'm the one who fell in love with a man in the mafia. The day we began to date my fate was sealed, whether I knew it at the time, or not. Whether we lasted as a couple, or not. It didn't matter. I was irrevocably tied to him.

Having now spent time with him and with Killian, I have come to learn the true definition of family. I lost mine young. Too young. I remember my parents. Remember loving them. But I also remember them being ambitious, and busy. They made little time for me. I don't blame them. I have done the same with my own career throughout the years.

When I lost them I had no one else. No true family until Tino came along. Then he was ripped from me and I was alone again.

Tino doesn't understand. He hasn't lost anyone the way I have. Even though he lost me, it wasn't the same. He thought I left him. That I wasn't in love, and didn't want to be a couple. It wasn't true I had to run. To stay away and fight for my life to go on.

The letter I was forced to leave, was a form of closure, even if it wasn't real. I didn't have that. For seven years the what-ifs plagued me.

Now I have him back, and his family needs help. Help I can provide. It's risky. There's a chance I won't survive this.

But if I do. When I do. I'll find a way to get him to forgive me. I'll make him understand.

As soon as this is done, Tino and I will be a family. In name with our marriage, and in blood as soon as I am pregnant. I rub my flat belly. We didn't use protection last night. I'm not on any sort of birth control. It's unlikely, but there is a chance. And if not this time, we will just keep trying.

In order for that future to come, we need to not be burdened with the fear of the Cartel on our doorstep. Our family will never know peace and happiness if we don't. I need that for Tino, to put his beast to rest, and to get back the future stolen from us.

He will forgive me, there is no doubt in my mind. But I'm sure my freedom will pay the price. I'd bet he's already making plans. He'll make it so I cannot leave the room without him because he needs me in his field of view. Probably won't be able to sit in my own chair either. He'll want to be touching me constantly. And since I left him handcuffed to the bed, I'm betting I will be on the receiving end of that for at least a few weeks.

It's a price I will happily pay, for I never want to be without him again anyway.

"Everything is ready." Killian says. I turn to him. Forgetting he was wrapping my knuckles for the fight while I was lost in my thought.

He and Ivan have assured me that they have enough men in the building in case of attack. Elena has assured me that she and Luna have my back and are monitoring our trackers in case any of us are taken.

The original plan called for Tino to be with Elena, but after they told me the story of him storming the house naked, with a piece of his headboard attached to wrist, I knew his beast was loose, that piece of Tino that craved blood, and vengeance and stop at nothing to get it. We can't risk him causing a scene, or calling an audible and ruining the plan. So for now, Tino is being forcibly detained in a van a few blocks away.

My monster, my beast is ready to storm the building at the first sign of trouble, and I love him all the more for it.

Grady enters the room and tells me it's time. I stand and do my usual pre-fight ritual of bouncing on my toes and getting my mind set on the task ahead. I don't know this opponent. Never seen him fight. It means I'm going to take a few hits before I can read what his weaknesses are.

We tap gloves, and immediately his fist swings out to my face. He's going to play dirty. I figured it was coming and was ready. I dodge it easily, but was not so lucky with his counter swing. It nails my ribs. Hard. Too hard. That's not just his hand he hit me with. He's got brass knuckles, or giant rings on his fingers.

Fuck. It's hard to breathe already after that hit. I shuffle back a few steps to buy myself a few precious seconds to let the adrenaline my body is releasing flow through me.

We go two rounds, each exchanging blows. With each passing minute I can see him slowing down. Problem is, so am I. The adrenaline isn't working anymore. My body is in too much pain.

I fight through it as best I can, and finally get him to his knees. Summoning any remaining energy I can pull, I roundhouse kick him. Lights out for him.

Then the lights go out for all of us.

Someone cut the power. Shit. This is the next stage of the plan, and I'm too tired to keep going. Just as predicted in our meeting, they grab me, tie me up and are hauling me away. I scream, kick, and fight, but I'm depleted. My body hurting. I don't stop. Can't. I need to make it back to Tino.

I swear I can hear him fighting his way through the crowds to get to me. Bullets are beginning to fly as a needle pierces my neck. My turn for lights out.

CHAPTER TWENTY-TWO

Val

You can't kill your brother. You can't kill your brother.

It has become my mantra tonight.

Sitting in this van is torture. Elena hacked the cameras and set up a monitor for me to watch. I don't know whether I want to thank her or curse her. Not being able to see her would have let my mind run rampant with horrible scenarios. Seeing it live, isn't far off what I could have imagined. She is taking a beating. I can see the blood and bruises through the shitty quality of the cameras. Every swing she takes is getting slower. And she's barely using her legs except to stand.

If no one kills this fucker before the night is out, I will be hunting him down.

The ten minutes she is in the ring feels like an eternity. My girl managed to get her opponent down. Knocked out. I'm so fucking proud of her. I'm ready to cheer, until the screen goes black. Massimo is with me as is Bosco. They are both trying to calm me down and hold me back. It's not working. Either the camera feed was cut, or the lights were. Either way, shit is going down and I need to get to my girl.

The ear piece in my ear rings with people barking at each other. I'm not fully listening as I run to the warehouse. There are key words I latch onto.

Elena says it wasn't the camera's someone cut the power. She was able to get it back on. "I'm sorry Val. I can't see her. She's not on camera. Her tracker signal is dead." I stop running. Coming to a dead stop in the middle of the street.

She's gone.

Someone needs to pay. I sprint the last half a block and enter into the chaos. Irish and Russian men are scrambling to contain the last few men. I jump into the fray. Swing my arms like wrecking balls and taking out men left and right. One guy pulls a gun on me. I get it out of his hand before he can blink. It would be too easy to shoot him. Instead I wrap my hands around his neck and lift. Squeezing and lifting, I can feel his pulse slowing. Right before it stops, I move my hands up to his chin and snap. When I release him, he falls to the ground. Never to move again.

"Val. Val can you hear me." It's Luca, and I don't care. This is all his fucking fault. She's gone because of his fucking plan.

Someone comes up to my shoulder and tries to shake me. Not caring who it is, I turn and swing. It was Killian. Good. He was also on board with this plan.

He gets back on his feet, and I ready my arm to swing again. Taking a step and throwing up his arms to block me, he says, "Luna says she's not dead. Or at least her tracker's not. When it's destroyed it sends a good-bye signal. Keira's never did. It cut off. Someone's blocking this signal. Which means there is a good probability that they are keeping her alive."

"You better be fucking right."

Luna and Elena continue to hunt for clues. We aren't sure how we missed them. We had every exit covered. Every road and alley in every direction watched. How the fuck did they slip past us?

Feeling like we're missing something, I go searching for my own clues. There are hallways and locked doors that no one has entered. I gather some men and tell them to begin breaking them open and searching.

We find a hidden staircase, one that goes down to a basement level where we find two dozen woman who are barely clothed, dirty, shivering, and several have glassy eyes, like they are high or were drugged. A team of our men work to get them out of their chains and brought up for medical attention.

As soon as they are able to talk, we will have Livianna speak to them, see if anyone of them know anything that could be useful to us. One of them may hold the key to finding my woman. Until then, I cannot look at my brother. Or my family. I get why they agreed to this. I get that Keira volunteered, but until she is safe in my arms, there is no calming my beast. He demands blood.

You cannot kill your brother.

You cannot kill your brother.

I continue searching the building, I find a second hidden staircase. This one leads up instead of down. I follow it to the top. To the roof. There is fresh blood smeared along the walls. Keira. She was leaving me a trail. I scan the rooftop looking for more clues. There are no stairs back down from here, it's too high to jump.

Helicopter. They are noisy as fuck but with gunfire to mask the sound, we wouldn't have heard it. And we didn't set up any surveillance for the fucking sky, only the streets.

"Luna." I say into my ear pierce.

"I'm working on finding her Val. I've got a signal booster code I am sending now to the NORAD satellite I hijacked."

"NORAD?" I can't help repeat it. This woman is fucking insane, and I couldn't appreciate her more right now. I give my head a shake. "How long with it take?"

"About six minutes."

"Can you check something else out while you wait?" I ask.

"Absolutely. What am I looking for?"

"See if you can find any flight plans for a helicopter in the area, or see if anyone reports seeing one. I'm on the roof. I've found blood. It's the only explanation I can think of." I'm practically begging at this point, and I don't care.

"Got it. Some fourteen year old posted a social media video of a low flying helicopter sixteen minutes ago two blocks from your location. I'm in Chicago air traffic control and see no authorized flight plans."

"Yes. That's her. I know it is. Can you track it?"

"Got a car?" She asks.

I don't respond. I run. I run so fast, I trip over my own feet a couple times. Bursting back into the main room, I spot Killian, Ivan, and Luca with Elena in a corner. I don't stop as I shout at them to move their asses. "Luna's found her." I scream.

They all come running with me. We pile into our cars and follow Luna's directions. She leads us to the shipyard. Beside me Killian growls. "He's got her on his fucking yacht."

"I thought that thing went up in flames?" Replies Grady as we commandeer two boats.

"It did. Sank to the bottom of the lake. He bought a new one last week through a shell company. Don't worry I'm draining those account now. He'll be broke in a matter of minutes." Claims Luna through our headset. "Satellite confirms, she's about three miles northwest of our location. Looks like the chopper is taking off again. She's not on it."

Ivan and his men are on one boat, they agree to follow the chopper. He's got more men on the main land following as close as they can up the coast. Hopefully they catch whoever is on it.

My focus is on Keira. On the yacht. It takes a few minutes for us to get there. When we do, I am the first one off the boat, and onto the yacht. "Keira!" I scream.

I search the deck I'm on, seeing no one. I move up to the next level. There is a body at the top of the stairs. I breathe a sigh of relief when I notice it isn't her. I call out again and again for her. Luca, and everyone else is on the lower decks doing the same. Finally I see movement ahead.

It's her. It's my Keira. She's alive.

She's is a bit more bruised and bloodied than I last saw her through the camera, but she is in one piece. There are three dead men around her, and she has a knife at the throat of another. It's Ramirez.

I run to her and drop to my knees. Ramirez's eyes are closed, but he's breathing. There is a dribble of blood on his neck from the knife. My girl looks like she's struggling to stay awake. I grip her face in my hands. "Keira." I say it softer this time.

Her eyes flicker to mine and she smiles. "Tino." She drops her gaze to Ramirez. "Got you an apology present."

I laugh. Full belly, head thrown back laugh. Behind me the rest of the family rushes up the steps.

"Holy fuck. Is that…" It's Massimo. He doesn't finish his sentence. We all recognize him. And my girl got him.

CHAPTER TWENTY-THREE

Keira

I wake up to my leg chained to the bottom of the bed, and my wrist with a handcuff around it. I follow the other end to find Tino laying propped up on his elbow, watching me. My Tino. My love. "Is it over?" I ask. My throat is dry and hoarse. It hurts to talk but I need to know.

"Mostly." He replies. "Our ranks are finally cleared. And an example was made out of those who betrayed the family. If there is anyone we missed, they won't be staying in the city long. And there is no place they can run where I won't find them."

"Killian?"

"His cousin escaped. But the seat is his. His father has officially named him his successor and their council has accepted it. He's going to have a fight on his hands. There are still those who may be loyal to his cousin working for him. And who knows when his cousin will reappear."

"We'll be there for him when he does. Right?"

"Yeah baby. We will."

"So...can we take this off now?" I ask shaking the handcuff.

"No." He replies. Then gently scoots me over so he can lay beside me. He falls asleep in moments. My poor guy.

I later learn I was out for nearly two days. He hadn't slept the entire time. He nearly resorted to peeing in bottles so he didn't leave my side. Thankfully Luca and their dad talked some sense into him.

Tino didn't let me leave the infirmary for a week after I woke up. Dr. Moro was a good sport even with me being a horrible patient. After a week though, I was done. So when Tino took us into the shower to wash us. Since I wasn't allowed to do it myself. I dropped to my knees and gave him the best blow job of his life. Afterwards, he didn't even bother to get either of us dressed before he stormed out of the bathroom. Honestly, I'm not even sure if he shut off the water. He paused momentarily by the bed to rip off the sheet and drape it over me. Mumbling something about how no one could see his wife.

As we climbed the stairs to the main floor I reminded him we weren't married yet. He said we were. He had hacked the courthouse system and filed our paperwork. I slapped at his back while he laughed. "You can't do that Tino. You're supposed to ask me to marry you."

"Nope." He replied simply.

"Nope?"

"Nope. We're married."

"And what if I wanted a real wedding? With a dress and flowers?" I argue back.

"Then, you'll have it." He said as he rounded the corner past the kitchen and towards the back stairs. "We can start planning after."

"After what?"

"After I knock you up."

"Val!" Hollers Livianna.

Then Massimo "Jesus Val! Get some clothes on."

I turn to look over my shoulder and see both he and Luca covering their wife's eyes. "Don't need clothes." He retorts as he starts up the stairs. "Need bed. Our bed." They all laughs.

As we get to the top I hear Livianna call after us. "Don't forget to feed and water your prisoner."

We get to the room and Tino throws me on the bed, then turns and goes back to the door. Shutting and locking it. Returning to me he crawls up the bed until his body covers mine. His erection pressing against my core. Moaning at the contact of our hot skin.

"Not asking you. Not giving you the chance to say no. We're married. You want a wedding, done. We'll start planning it. You want a honeymoon, we'll go for a month. You want a house, I'll tell my guys to start building. The only thing I won't give you is space." He buries his head in my shoulder. "Lost you for seven years the first time, then two hours the second. Can't do it again."

"Tino..." Tears sting my eyes at his admission.

"You're mine."

"I'm yours." I say with as much conviction and love as I can pour into my voice.

"Good." Then his mouth is on me.

I don't need a proposal, I just wanted to tease him. His beast is calm, but that doesn't mean I can't bring him out to play with me when the mood strikes.

Also By Nova Mason

CARUSO FAMILY MAFIA
RUNNING - Luca and Elena
HUNTING - Massimo and Livianna
FIGHTING - Val and Keira

COMING SOON - DOYLE IRISH MOB
CUTTING - AVAILABLE FOR PRE-SALE
RIPPING
TEARING

FOLLOWED BY - VASILIEV BRATVA
CLASHING
BATTLING
WARRING

About the Author

Nova Mason made her debut with her first novel "Running: Caruso Mafia Book One". The series continued with Massimo's story in "Hunting", and then Val's in "Fighting". She fell in love with books while still in the womb and learned to read at only three. Her goal as a kid was to read every book in the children's section of the local library one shelf at a time. Sadly they remodeled before she could complete her goal and lost ability to track her progress. Now she's working to fill the library in her house with books she loves and a shelf or two dedicated to her own stories.

She loves hearing from her readers, so please don't hesitate to drop her a note on one of her social media sites.

Printed in Great Britain
by Amazon

43043984R00091